For Nan

1

Old Mamm Spriggan sleeps under a blanket of leaves, curled like a seed, tight as a secret. Now and then she twitches out a gnarly leg. Sometimes her long twig fingers scratch her head, dislodging a millipede burrowing in her brain. For days and nights through rain and shine she slumbers, giving herself back to the land until she's needed.

While she sleeps her mind fills with rotting things: mulch and manure, maggots and mould, putrid fluids and pungent juices reeking with the sweet-rich tang of decay. She dreams of the spinning Earth and scudding clouds, sunrise and moonbeams, cycles and seasons, longing for a time when she wasn't the last of her kind.

Best of all, is when she dreams of the girl.

She hugs herself with rough bark arms and grins when she thinks of the child's long auburn hair and eyes the colour of a mountain lake. How she'd like to taste those eyes. Pluck them out and roll them between her fingers, feel them slide cool and juicy down her throat.

Mamm can't remember exactly when she was last called into life, for time disintegrates quickly when you're in the ground, but she recalls that long hot summer week as if it happened only yesterday. The girl's trespass had caused her to wake in the usual way – the angry dark magic filling her with fury and summoning her to protect the glade. Her heart had beaten raw and ravenous with cruelty, yet she had only watched the child.

The girl was nothing like the others who'd been foolish enough to enter her domain. She dug her hands into the crumble-soft soil and laughed when a spider crawled up her arm. She swam the river in a thunderstorm and climbed the broken oak tree at night. She skipped through dew-wet grass and spun in circles, giddy on the magic of dawn.

Few humans were able to see Old Mamm, yet the girl had. If only the child had spoken to her that night. If only there was a way to get close to her . . .

Turning over, she wheezes a raspy chuckle then buries her face into the dirt and murmurs excitedly to the earthworms, 'Next time she'll speak to me, I'll make sure of it. Next time she'll be mine.'

2

They'd been driving for hours and it was dark by the time they entered the forest. Pippa Newton pressed her cheek to the car window and surveyed the storm-ravaged sky. A tunnel of trees arched overhead, their long bare branches interlaced like skeletal fingers in the silvery moonlight. In one of them sat a crow, its feathers slick with rain. It turned its head as they drove by and Pippa shivered. There was something unkind in its gaze, something that reminded her of another set of hungry black eyes. It was a memory that belonged to a nightmare, yet she hadn't been dreaming when she'd seen them.

Pippa adjusted her baseball cap and slumped down in the seat. She told herself she was being silly – whatever she *thought* she'd seen that night couldn't have been real – when the car lurched. Dad ran his hand over his bald head then thumped the steering wheel. 'Look at the state of this road! That's if you can call it a road.' His mood worsened with every pothole they encountered. Each jolt and bump shook loose a new complaint. 'Of all the places to live, it had to be Cornwall. Why anyone would want to live in the woods . . .'

'I think it's romantic,' said Pippa's mum, turning round to grin at Pippa and her big brother. 'I'd love to live in the middle of the forest. No noisy traffic, or alarms going off, or people making a racket outside Tesco Express.' Pushing up her thick auburn fringe so it looked as if she had no hair, she winked at the children. Sure enough, Dad took the bait. He complained for three minutes straight about how living in the woods was uncivilised before noticing his wife was pulling faces and mimicking him as he spoke.

'Yes, OK. You've made your point. I'm just an old grump.' He pretended to be offended then laughed. 'Who needs a decent Wi-Fi connection, hey, Jed?'

Pippa hoped her brother might join in the conversation, but as usual he was staring at the Switch console glued to his hands, his brow furrowed in concentration.

'Look, Jed!' she said, pointing outside. When he didn't answer, she tugged out one of his earbuds.

'What?' he snapped.

'We're in the forest. Aren't you excited?'

'Yeah, great.'

Pippa sighed. A few months ago he couldn't wait to play in the woods.

She watched a gust of wind shake the bone-thin tree trunks and thought about the last time they'd stayed. It had been summer and the trees were alive with birdsong, the long grass home to an army of frogs, and the ground teeming with insects. She and Jed had played outside every day, climbing trees, making dens and building a tree house. Now it was autumn and an eerie white mist hung in the air. It made the woods feel even more magical.

Pippa opened the window and took a deep breath. As she inhaled the enticing pine scent of the forest she felt her mood improve. Jed was bound to cheer up in a day or two; going away together could be just what they needed.

'Do you have to? It's freezing!' moaned Jed.

'But I want some air.'

'There's air in the car, otherwise we'd all be dead.'

He looked at her expectantly and the tiny muscles of his cheek twitched, making his left eye squint. He was thirteen, two years older than her, and he'd had the facial tic for as long as she could remember. Most of the time she barely noticed it, but when he was angry or embarrassed it became more pronounced.

He tugged her baseball cap down over her eyes then reached over and closed the window. 'You know I don't like the cold,' he muttered.

Pippa fought the urge to snatch his Switch from him and throw it outside. See how he liked *that*. Ever since she'd started at Manning Park High he'd been moody with her. He tolerated her at home, but in school he acted like she didn't exist. He wouldn't let her enter the main gates with him, and if he saw her in the corridor he'd walk the other way. Mum said he was growing up and was just being a teenager. If that were true, she didn't much like the person he was becoming.

They drove down the long dirt track that led to Grandpa's house for several minutes, then Dad stopped the car and twisted round in his seat. 'Right, kids, out you get.'

Jed folded his arms and Pippa felt her stomach flip the way it did when they went too fast over a bump in the road.

'Come on, love,' said Mum, reaching over and patting Jed's knee. 'It's only for a week. It will fly by and when you get back—'

'I'll have a nice new house I don't want to live in, and a nice new school I don't—' He stopped and stared out of the window as if he couldn't bring himself to finish the sentence.

Dad gave him a pained smile. 'You know why we're moving, Jed. The new restaurant is just round the corner, so it means I can be at home more. It'll take a while to adjust, but it will be for the best. You'll see.'

Jed rolled his eyes and said nothing.

The plan was for them to stay at Grandpa's for half-term while their parents moved into their new place. Dad thought saying goodbye to their old house might be upsetting for them and said their grandfather could use the company. Pippa knew Jed was unhappy because there was no Wi-Fi or phone signal in the forest, which meant he couldn't play Xbox with his friends, but there were other things they could do: like go on walks or visit Ollie, the boy who lived down the lane. Maybe they could use the present she got for her birthday – a pair of night-vision binoculars that recorded video. She'd already filmed foxes at home and couldn't wait to try them out in the woods.

Dad frowned. 'Jed, please get out of the car.'

Pippa braced herself for Jed to refuse, and an argument to start, when Mum began tapping her fist against her forehead, each time changing her expression – angry, shocked, sad, confused, happy – and then stuck out her tongue and crossed her eyes.

Jed sighed, but Pippa giggled. Mum had done this

since they were little and although it was silly, it always cheered her up.

They exited the car, Dad taking their bags out of the boot while Mum hugged them. 'I'm going to miss you guys. Be good for Grandpa.'

'Always,' said Pippa.

Glancing about the garden, she felt a shiver of excitement. In front of the house was an overgrown lawn with a broken oak tree that had been struck by lightning, and beyond that was a line of laurel bushes that surrounded the glade, called Whispering Hollow. In the centre was a large flat stone that lay on top of two smaller ones, hiding an entranceway into the earth that was just big enough to crawl through. No one knew who'd put the stones there or why, but Grandpa said it had probably been there since Neolithic times. They weren't allowed inside as the ground was unsafe, but just knowing it was there – *forbidden* – was thrilling.

Following the others, she walked towards Grandpa's house. The little cottage had always been a bit ramshackle, the roof sloping at an odd angle and ivy choking the windows. Now it looked smaller than ever, as if it had sunk in on itself.

Dad knocked on the small wooden door. 'Hello, anyone there?'

The house remained stubbornly silent.

'I can't see a light on. You did tell him we were coming?' asked Mum.

'I left a message on his answerphone.'

Mum looked incredulous. 'So you didn't actually talk to him?'

'I called back yesterday but couldn't get through. Probably a fault on the line; that's what happens when you live in the middle of nowhere.' Dad added a little too firmly, 'He'll be pleased to see them, don't worry. You get in the car. I won't be long.'

'We've driven all this way. Surely we can stop for a cup of tea?'

Dad rubbed the back of his neck. 'It's already late and we still have packing to do.'

Mum smiled sympathetically. 'I know it's hard, but you have to talk to him about the future at some point. What if he has another fall? He can't carry on living here, it's too remote.'

'Try telling *him* that! I'll have that conversation with him when we collect the kids, I promise, but not now. I'm stressed enough with the move and opening the new restaurant. Please, darling.'

Mum sighed as if there was no point arguing. 'OK. He's your father. You know best.' She cuddled the children again and covered their faces in kisses. Jed squirmed and pretended to be annoyed, but Pippa hugged her back fiercely. As much as she loved Grandpa, a week without her parents was a long time.

Dad waited until Mum had returned to the car, then hammered on the door like he was trying to break it down.

'Maybe he can't hear us,' suggested Pippa.

'Or he doesn't *want* to hear us,' scoffed Jed. 'You know what happened last time.'

Pippa walked round the side of the house. She was looking forward to staying and didn't want to spoil it by remembering how their previous visit had ended.

As she passed the window to her left, she saw something that made her gasp. Several large dark shapes were hanging inside the room, suspended from the ceiling. They were as big as fully grown men, with looped heads, thin bodies, and long arms and legs. Looking closer, she realised they were woven from willow branches.

She scanned the windows upstairs and shuddered to see more of the strange figures. There was something disturbingly familiar about them, yet she couldn't remember seeing them before. Who would make such creepy things? And where was Grandpa? He didn't go out much, not since his accident.

Dad banged on the door again. 'I told you we were coming today!'

Pippa was starting to worry something bad might have happened when they heard the clang of bolts being drawn.

'Finally,' said Dad.

The door creaked open and Grandpa appeared. He'd grown a patchy white beard since she'd last seen him and was thinner and more hunched over. Worst of all were his eyes. Like the house, they were dark and empty and had a haunted look about them. He glanced nervously between Dad and the children.

'I told you when I took them home last time . . .' he croaked.

'It's only for a week. They won't be any trouble,' said Dad.

The moon peeped out from behind a cloud, casting a shaft of silvery light across the doorway, and Grandpa shrank back.

'Kids, give us a moment, would you?' asked Dad.

They reluctantly turned and moved a dozen paces back, but as soon as her father wasn't looking, Pippa crept towards them again. She knew it was wrong to eavesdrop, but she'd never been good at obeying rules. Like at school when they were warned not to climb the giant conker tree in the playground. Pippa told her teacher she'd scaled much higher trees, but he didn't seem interested. To prove her point, she climbed it one lunchtime. When he saw her standing in its leafy branches he became *very* interested, but not in a good way.

Dad spoke in a shouted whisper. 'I know you said—'

Grandpa held up his hand, stopping him mid-sentence. 'It's not safe for the children any more. There are things—'

'Of course it's safe!' Dad let out a heavy breath. 'It's just superstitious nonsense, and you know it!'

Pippa strained to listen, but couldn't catch his reply. Grandpa had a tendency to mumble and wasn't easy to understand thanks to his Cornish accent. He'd lived in the forest for as long as she could remember and had always liked having them stay before. All she knew was that everything had changed the last time they were here, the night she'd had the nightmare.

Sensing her father would turn round soon, Pippa hurried back over to Jed. A moment later, Dad spun on his heels and stalked towards them. 'Love you, Newt,' he said, squeezing her shoulder. He held his arm out towards Jed, who swerved from his reach. Dad looked hurt but smiled weakly, seemingly resigned to the rejection. 'Behave yourselves.'

'But he said we can't stay!' exclaimed Jed. Pippa raised an eyebrow at her brother. Had he been eavesdropping too?

Dad jumped into the car and started the engine.

'Mum!' called Pippa, waving her arm.

Their mother smiled, unaware of the conversation that had just taken place, and waved at them as the car drove away. The children stared down the empty driveway then turned back to the house. Grandpa was gripping the doorframe as if his legs might buckle. It wasn't like he could take them home – he wasn't able to drive since he'd fallen over and hurt his knee. As if admitting defeat, he held out his arms for a hug, but Pippa could tell he wasn't really focused on them. His eyes were scanning the darkness as if afraid of what might be out there.

3

If Grandpa's house looked neglected from the outside, it was nothing compared to the inside. The hallway was full of dead leaves and pine cones as if the forest had blown in through the open door. The wallpaper was black with mould and there was a column of brown, slimy mushrooms growing up the wall.

It wasn't just the house that was a shambles. Grandpa's hair was like a bird's nest and his jumper was on inside out.

He hurriedly bolted the door then turned back to them and coughed. 'I try to keep on top of things, but...'

Pippa looked around in shock, then touched his arm. 'We're here now, we can help.'

Grandpa's eyes glistened with tears. It seemed like he was going to say something, but then he limped off towards the kitchen. Maybe he was embarrassed by the state of the place and that's why he didn't want them here. Pippa knew her father cared about Grandpa, even if the two of them didn't always get on, but he really should have stopped for a cup of tea. If he'd come inside, he'd have seen how much Grandpa was struggling.

Jed took out his phone. 'No reception, as usual.'

Pippa picked up the telephone from the hallway table. There was no dial tone. 'It's not working.'

'That's weird,' said Jed. 'How did Dad leave a message if it's not working?'

Pippa shrugged. They shared a worried look then walked down the hallway and glanced into the living room on their right. The sofa and armchairs were covered with leaves. Jed frowned, the muscles of his left cheek twitching. 'Don't worry, Newt. We'll help him get the place sorted.' Pippa nodded and managed a tiny smile. Jed might be moody sometimes, but it was a relief to have him with her.

They followed their grandfather into the kitchen and looked around wide-eyed. Forest debris covered every surface: the countertops, the table, even the wooden dresser was thick with dirt and pine needles. A bracken plant grew out of a teapot on one shelf, while moss covered the cups and saucers on another. A milk jug had been knocked over; inside it was the skull of a mouse. Black feathers littered a pile of plates as if a crow had been helping itself to scraps.

Pippa bit her fingernail and took an uncertain step back. Grandpa's house had always been cosy and welcoming, a place where she felt happy and safe, but now she barely recognised it.

Then Pippa saw something that made her body tense. Hanging above the sink was a row of twig men. They were smaller than the ones she'd seen from outside, but otherwise the same. Each one was attached to the ceiling with a length of twine. They were made crudely, their spindly arms and legs peculiarly long. Again she wondered where she had seen them before.

Feeling light-headed, she gripped the back of a chair and surveyed the wooden table before her. It was hard to believe she'd sat there and drawn pictures a few months ago. Now it was covered with half-formed twig men. Pippa went to pick one up.

'Don't!' shouted Grandpa. She startled and he said more softly, 'It's best not to touch the things they make.'

'Who makes?' asked Jed, his eyes boggling at the chaos around them.

Grandpa turned his back to them and wiped a layer of green slime from the kettle like it was perfectly normal. 'You've had a long journey. I'll make you some hot chocolate and something to eat.'

Pippa stood next to him and watched as he picked up a mug. A shiny black beetle tumbled out of it and scuttled across the countertop, then crawled over her thumb.

'Hello there,' she whispered to it, gently lifting her hand and letting it run across her fingers before lowering it back down.

Grandpa opened the door to the pantry – a tiny room filled with shelves of food, and came out holding a loaf of bread. Then he filled the toaster and wiped some plates.

Pippa's eyes darted once more to the hanging figures. 'Who makes them, Grandpa?' she asked.

Either his hearing had got worse, or he was ignoring the question.

Pippa brushed a mound of wet leaves from a chair and sat down. Her gaze returned to the figures in the window and she found herself thinking about the nightmare she'd had. A body made from branches had been buried in the ground. She'd sensed it stirring beneath the earth, its limbs slowly moving. A shudder ran through her as she recalled how a single twig hand had poked up from a pile of leaves like the dead coming back to life.

'Are you OK?' asked Jed. 'You've gone pale.'

Pippa rubbed her arms. 'I was thinking about . . .' She paused, changing her mind about what she was going to say. 'I'm just worried about Grandpa living here on his own.' She hadn't told Jed or anyone else about her nightmare, or what she'd seen when she'd woken up. It wasn't just that he wouldn't believe her. If she didn't talk or think about it, she could almost convince herself that she'd imagined it.

Grandpa handed them each a plate of toast and a steaming mug of hot chocolate, then sat down on a chair without bothering to brush off the leaves first. A sticky film covered the bottom of the plate and Pippa wrinkled her nose, unsure whether it was wise to eat anything. She was about to ask again who'd made the twig men, when he gave them a meaningful look.

'You know I love you both. Always have, always will.'

Pippa and Jed nodded.

He smiled. 'You're good'uns, the both of you, so I know you'll do as you're told. While you're here, you must promise to stay out of the forest.'

Pippa spluttered on her drink. 'But, Grandpa, why?'

'I'm sorry. It's for your own safety.'

'But I was going to use my night-vision binoculars to record animals!'

Grandpa raised his hand. 'This is important.'

Pippa stared at him in disbelief. She was desperate to film woodland wildlife. The only things she saw in London were grey squirrels and scrawny foxes.

Grandpa folded his arms and her hopes frizzled to nothing.

'Couldn't we go if you came too?' asked Jed.

Pippa felt a tug of love for her brother. Jed had no interest in going into the woods these days. As long as he had a screen to look at he was happy.

'Yes,' said Pippa, jumping on the idea. 'What if you came too? Please!'

Grandpa shook his head. 'Not even if I come with you. And it goes without saying you're to stay away from the glade.'

Pippa felt the sting of a tear. It was Grandpa who'd inspired her love of nature in the first place. They'd never been allowed in Whispering Hollow, but Grandpa had often taken them into the forest when they were little. If they were quiet, he said they might see something magical. Jed got bored within a few minutes, but Pippa would sit with him for hours. Somehow the birdsong was sweeter than in London and the grass a more vivid shade of green. There were more animals too: not just foxes, but badgers, deer, owls, bats, mice. Once a robin had landed on her leg and a squirrel had eaten a nut from her hand.

They were allowed in the woods before, so why not now? She'd only gone into Whispering Hollow once, and there was no way he could know. If he'd found out he would have told her off in summer, not waited until now.

Pippa crossed the room and took her binoculars from her bag. She showed them to Grandpa and held up her book about wildlife habitats and the best times to see them. Grandpa wasn't listening. He was staring at the twig men in the window. A cold breeze swept through the house as if the door had been left open, and for a moment the figures seemed to dance.

'It's time you went up to your rooms,' said Grandpa. 'Off you go now.' He spoke without taking his eyes from the window.

The children glanced at one another and then back to the figures. They were still now, yet a moment ago they'd appeared almost alive.

'Come on, Newt,' muttered Jed. He picked up their bags and headed to the door.

But Pippa didn't want to go to bed. She wanted to find out who'd made the twig men and why they couldn't go into the forest. 'How am I going to record any wildlife?' she complained.

'I don't know. Find another hobby,' he said, thrusting her bag at her. When she didn't move, he shoved her out the door.

'One more thing,' Grandpa shouted after them as they walked up the stairs. 'Rodents have been coming into the house at night. If you hear anything, wake me up.'

The children each had their own bedroom when they came to stay, located across the landing from one another. Jed went straight to his room, but Pippa paused outside her door. She wasn't afraid of much – not small spaces, or spiders, or getting a detention for climbing trees. But going into the place where she'd seen something scary in the middle of the night was different.

Gathering her courage, she opened the door and switched on the light. Her heart skipped a beat. The room was full of twig men. Several hung above the window and there were two more dangling at the foot of her bed. They were big – easily the same size as her. Pippa clenched her fists and looked around. All her things were there: the wooden desk with the microscope that Grandpa had bought her, the tall shelving unit with her nature books and large glass jars containing feathers and dried flowers, and her bed strung with fairy lights. Everything was cosy and familiar, but it felt different. She'd spent so many happy hours here. It wasn't fair to have it ruined by those *things*.

She startled as Jed appeared at her elbow.

'They're in my room too,' he said. 'Why do you think Grandpa makes them?'

'He didn't. He said not to touch the things *they* make.'

Jed raised his eyebrows. 'Come on, it's obvious he's the one making this stuff. That's why he didn't answer when we asked him about it. Pine cones and bracken don't just spring up in your house. He must be bringing them inside.'

'But why?'

Jed shrugged. 'Why drive us home in the middle of the night?'

Pippa tried not to think about the last time they'd stayed, how she'd woken from her nightmare to see a hideous woman with a sackcloth for a head and limbs made from branches crouched on her windowsill. Or the look of fear on Grandpa's face when she'd told him.

A group of moths fluttered haphazardly around the light above them. Pippa watched them for a moment then grabbed the leg of the nearest twig man and yanked. She pulled down another and

23

another, forming a heap of broken bodies under the window. The light flickered as if it might go out, and Jed stiffened.

'I'm going to play Mario Kart in my room. Want to join me?' he asked.

Pippa shook her head. 'I'm tired. Think I'll go to bed.'

Jed's face dropped, his expectant smile replaced with a frown. But he didn't leave the room, so Pippa decided to ask a question. 'Why are you so upset about moving? Is it because you don't want to change school? I'll be there too, so it's not like you won't know anyone.'

Jed pulled a face, as if the fact she was going to be there made it worse.

Pippa tried not to feel hurt. They'd always talked before, and she wasn't that keen on moving school herself. She'd only been at Manning Park for a couple of months, but she'd already made friends and she liked her teachers.

'You can tell me,' she said. 'I promise I won't say anything to Mum and Dad.'

Jed shuffled his feet. 'There's nothing to tell.'

Unsure what to say, Pippa lifted Jed's arm and brought his hand to his forehead. It was something they did sometimes, a game like the one Mum played. Each time his hand touched his head, he had to change

24

expression: sad, angry, happy. He went along with it, pulling different faces until he went cross-eyed, and they both laughed. But his smile faded quickly and Pippa's heart dropped. If only he'd tell her what was wrong, maybe she could help.

She didn't want him to leave just yet, so she searched for something else to say.

'Can you help me with my binoculars? I can't get the video to record in infrared.'

'Really, now?'

She nodded and pulled them from her bag. Jed tried a few different switches. 'It would help if you still had the instructions.' He played around some more then gave up and handed them back to her. 'What is it with you and these binoculars anyway?'

'When I grow up I want to be a camerawoman and film nature documentaries.'

Jed raised his eyebrows.

It was true she'd changed her mind a few times. Last month, she'd wanted to be a marine biologist and study whales, and before that she'd wanted to be a ranger and work on a wildlife park in Africa. Or look after the penguins at London Zoo, she wasn't sure.

'High-resolution cameras are the reason we know so much about animals,' she told him. 'Do you know why hummingbirds hum?'

'Because they forgot the words?'

Pippa tutted. 'They hum because they've got a pair of tiny wings that are whipping back and forth forty times every second. And we know that because someone recorded it on camera.'

'Really, forty times?' he asked.

Pippa nodded.

'Strange. That's *exactly* how many times a second you annoy me.'

She jabbed him in the side and he shoved her back.

'Night, Newt,' he said. 'Don't let the twig men bite.'

Laughing, she closed the door. One of the moths flying around the room landed on her arm. 'Well, aren't you beautiful?' she said. The insect fluttered its fragile grey wings as if agreeing, then took to the air once more. As it danced around the ceiling, the light bulb fizzed and flickered. Unlike her brother, Pippa had never been afraid of the dark, not even when she was little, so the thought of the light going out didn't worry her. She wasn't about to lose sleep over a few twigs either.

She was walking over to the window to close the curtains when something outside caught her attention. A shadowy figure darted out from the woods and ran between the compost heap and the shed at the bottom of the garden.

She lifted the binoculars to her face. A foggy gloom hung over the ground, making it hard to see. Moving the tiny dial on the side, she watched as the grainy image became a little clearer. Holding her breath, she scanned from left to right and back again. The garden was still. Not a breeze stirred the trees. It must have been a fox or a badger, the moon lengthening its shadow to make it look like a person. Her shoulders dropped with relief. Of course it was. What else could it have been?

4

Old Mamm Spriggan wakes from a deep rain-soaked sleep and finds herself lacking. Where her torso should be are hollow ribs, her xylophone bones picked clean by birds. A pile of loose branches and half-rotten twine is all that remains of her left leg. Her other is missing a pine cone knee and three twig toes. Cautiously, she lifts one diseased yew arm and then the other. She's fallen apart and remade herself so many times she can barely recall her last form. She wants to touch her face, but is worried she might not recognise what she finds.

Something skitters in her chest – the tiny feet of a rodent scrabbling to escape her rib cage, or the quickening calling her into life, she can't be sure. Her mind feels bloated, her thoughts edgeless and velvet soft. How long did she sleep? She tries to fathom the depth of her forgetting, but can find no bottom to it. Cursing herself for falling down the rabbit hole of her dreams, she cracks her knuckles and takes a deep breath.

Bringing both hands to her eyeless face, she feels the shape of her head: a tatty hessian sack pulled tight over a wicker cage. Ah yes, now she remembers. Feeling a little more like herself, she wipes the moss from her pelvis and sniffs the chilly air. Her favourite season: autumn. She grins at the thought of jewel-red plums oozing sticky wasp sap, crab apples with wrinkled skin and tart flesh, and rich-ripe pears, their bodies bruised and soft with rot.

A wood-boring beetle gnaws at her elbow. She shakes it away and tries to sit up, but she's not strong enough. She tries to blink but she has no eyes. Lying on her back, she gropes the forest floor. Finding nothing but dirt and pine needles, she reaches further. Tiny branches untwist and pull apart with a crack as her arm extends, spreading like the roots of a tree.

An acorn rolls towards her. She snatches it up with a triumphant chuckle and lodges it where an eye should be. It sways on its stalk but holds firm. Peering into the gloomy bracken, she spots another acorn to her right. She places it where her other eye should be then finds two small bay leaves for eyelids. She shifts on to her side and stinking liquid pours from her belly in a gurgling gush. A ball of moss rolls towards her and she quickly pokes the spongy mass into the cavity of her stomach.

She sits up and the forest brings her more treasures. Mushrooms sprout from the earth, their bulbous grey caps pleasingly firm to the touch. She fingers their silky underside, enjoying their wrinkled folds, then picks them and stuffs them into her head. Able to think more clearly, she clicks her fingers. On the housing estate next to the forest, shed doors fly open with a bang. Garden debris rolls over the earth towards her: twine, a shard of terracotta pot, sackcloth, rope. She sorts through them greedily, picking out the things she needs.

Finally, she scoops up an armful of festering fruit and packs it into her body. Quince cysts and blackberry clots coagulate in her pot belly. Relieved to have soft innards, she releases a satisfied sigh.

She pushes herself up from the forest floor then staggers to one side. She feels light and insubstantial, as hollow as the rushes by the riverbank and as weak as a baby blackbird. Like a foul mood, a good strong wind could blow her clean away.

Water drips from the dense undergrowth with a tip-tap splash, the ground all ache and heave. She pushes aside a thicket of bracken, its long fronds glistening with glutinous globs of liquid, and carefully lifts one leg. The earth sucks at her greedily, gulps and pops. She shakes her foot but the mud clings fast, as if the land doesn't want to let her go.

Her heart thuds with panic. *No.* The ground can't reclaim her – not yet.

Placing her hands on her knees, she leans forward and convulses like a wet dog, shaking off her fear with the dirt. Feeling a little better, she straightens up and knocks the side of her head. A cloud of dust and dried insect husks spews from her left ear, followed by a bluebottle that buzzes about her face, unhappy to be evicted from its home.

The tiny acorns dangling in her eye sockets sway as she walks, unsteady on her bramble-bound feet. Her mouth is a soft bruised plum, the flesh rotten and split, ruby juice trickling down her chin. She wipes it with the back of her hand as she pushes through the bracken, then emerges and blinks in the silvery moonlight. She never knows where she might fall apart, or how long for, and is surprised to find herself on the edge of the forest.

The glade – she must return.

The thought stings at her, nettle sharp. Flailing her arms, she crashes through the woods, disturbing a family of mice who had just settled down for the evening and irritating a barn owl who had made plans for them. *That's it, faster now, Old Mamm.* Laughter builds at the back of her throat, remembering how it feels to swing her limbs, remembering how it feels to be alive.

A loud chortle bursts from her lips and dozens of crows flap their wings and take to the air, their harsh cries sending a flock of starlings barrelling up into the navy-dark. Hundreds of them swoop through the sky, their bodies forming a twisting, turning cloud of black. Rabbits and voles and deer bolt into the undergrowth. A squirrel crosses her path and freezes in alarm, before scampering up a tree. On the nearby estate, dogs whine and cats cower behind sofas. All animals hide when they sense her coming, though she means them no harm.

She likes to think of herself as the spark that starts the forest fire, the lightning strike. Unpredictable, destructive, necessary even, but never welcome. No, she's never that.

She reaches the clearing and darts across the garden. There's a face at the window: the girl. Pausing by the shed, she blinks up at the child haloed in golden light. She wants to clap her hands and sing, she wants to bite and tear and kill things. Mamm knows she has no choice; she must frighten the girl away. Yet how can she? The child saw her. What if . . . ?

Clutching her belly, she gasps as her newly made innards crumble to dust. It feels like someone took a spoon and hollowed her clean out. A yawning chasm of need opens up inside her and she aches, she aches, she aches with it.

The child is her only hope. Whatever it takes, the girl must speak to her.

Old Mamm must know her name.

5

Pale grey light filtered around the edges of Pippa's curtains, telling her it would soon be dawn. Remembering where she was, she stretched out her limbs and smiled. She could use her binoculars and . . . Last night crashed over her like an icy wave and she groaned and thumped her pillow. She wasn't allowed in the woods.

Scritch-scratch.

Pippa sat up and looked around the shadowy room.

There it was again: a faint scratching, scurrying sound. She peered at the floor, half expecting to see a rat running along the skirting boards, but there was nothing.

Scritch-scratch.

She scrambled out of bed and switched on the light, then checked under her desk. There was no pink nose and shivering white whiskers looking back at her. She went to the wardrobe and got on her hands and knees, but the only things beneath it were balls of dust. Pippa couldn't help feeling a little disappointed. She loved rats and had often asked her parents if she could have one as a pet.

Thud.

A pile of books toppled from the bookcase, nearly landing on her head. Whatever it was must be big to do that. More scurrying – first to her left and then to her right.

She stood up, her gaze jumping from one wall to the next. A glass jar lay across the base of her microscope, the seashells it contained now strewn across her desk. The lampshade next to it was lopsided, as if something had knocked into it, and her collection of feathers were no longer neatly arranged on the shelf but littered over her books.

She stepped back and was surprised to see the twig men at her feet. She could still make out the looped shapes of their heads and long arms and legs, even though they were all jumbled up. They reminded her of puppets with their strings cut.

Wait.

Didn't she leave them under the window? Why were they by her bed?

Pippa's mouth went dry. For a moment, she imagined them coming to life and creeping around her while she slept. No, that was ridiculous. She'd been tired and must have remembered wrong. Or Jed or Grandpa had moved them. Nothing sinister had been prowling around her room in the night. There were rats in the house, that's all.

Large, invisible rats.

After a final check of her room, she dressed and went downstairs. The kitchen looked even dirtier than she remembered. Piles of wet leaves were heaped by the back door and under the table. The mushrooms growing up the doorframe seemed to have grown bigger in the night, some as big as dinner plates, and every surface was thick with earth and pine needles. Her shoulders dropped. She wanted to spend the day outside, not stuck indoors. It would take hours to clean this lot up.

Grandpa shuffled about, humming as he put bread into the moss-covered toaster. He was wearing the same clothes as yesterday, his jumper still inside out with the label at the front. He greeted her the way he always did in the mornings: dipping his head and tipping a pretend hat. The familiarity of it filled her with happiness, yet it made her feel sad too. It reminded her of other times they'd visited, when things had been better.

Jed was sitting at the table wearing an oversized

black hoodie and a thick grey scarf. He didn't usually get up this early; maybe he'd been woken by a noise too? She would've asked him, but he was playing on his Switch and would be cross if she distracted him. In summer they'd chatted over breakfast about how they were going to build a den or a tree house. Now he didn't raise his head as she sat down. He didn't even lift his eyes from the screen as he picked up some toast.

Opening his mouth to take a bite, he stopped and stared at his plate in disgust – or, more precisely, the large black spider strolling across it. Pippa picked it up, admiring its long hairy legs, before placing it on a pile of leaves on the floor. Jed glared at her, as if her actions were as offensive to him as the spider's existence.

'Why didn't you put it outside? It shouldn't be in the house.'

'Actually, spiders were here first and have the right to go wherever they want. They've been around for nearly four hundred million years.'

'Yet they *still* haven't figured out where the door is.'

Pippa searched her brains for a comeback, and would no doubt have come up with something clever, but just then Grandpa distracted her by opening the fridge door. He sniffed the bottle of milk in his hand. 'Still fresh!' he said to no one in particular.

Placing three mugs of tea on the table, he took a seat next to Pippa. Then he picked up a spoon and dipped it into the sugar bowl, tasting it with the tip of his tongue. Nudging her with his elbow, he grinned and whispered, 'Still sweet.' Pippa shifted in her seat. She was used to Grandpa making up games, but wasn't sure she got the joke. Should she join in? Eat some toast and say, *still crunchy*? Or sniff the strawberry jam and say, *still fruity*?

Thankfully Grandpa didn't state the obvious about any more breakfast items and asked them about school instead. What was their favourite subject? What did they want to do when they grew up? Jed shrugged and gave one-word answers. Pippa didn't do much better. She would have told him that biology was her favourite subject, but she didn't see the point in telling him about how she wanted to film wildlife one day when she wasn't allowed to go in the woods.

CREAK.

The back door opened slowly, letting in a rush of cold air and making the leaves swirl across the floor. Pippa got up and closed it. When she turned back, Grandpa was holding on to the edge of the table, his knuckles white.

'It's just the wind,' she said.

Grandpa muttered something she couldn't catch.

Normally she loved his quirky sense of humour, but he was starting to unsettle her. He still hadn't told them who'd made the twig men. She desperately wanted to ask, but she had to pick the right moment.

'Grandpa,' she said softly, laying a hand on his arm. He didn't reply. She glanced at Jed for help, but he was jabbing at the controls of his Switch with his earbuds in. Unsure what to do, she raised her voice and found herself saying, 'You know your jumper's on inside out and back to front?' Grandpa looked up at her, his pale-blue eyes brimming with anxiety.

Then his expression changed, and there was a flicker of something like hope.

'Out inside it's know I,' he said with a smile. Then he added, 'Too backwards speak you.'

Pippa giggled. They'd played word games a few times, though they'd never spoken backwards before. She took a moment to think and said, 'Straight it put?'

He nodded, which she took to mean *no*.

'Out inside yours turn,' he said.

She repeated his words in her head and grinned when she understood. 'On are you,' she said, taking off her jumper and putting it on backwards and inside out.

Jed looked up and Grandpa gestured for him to take out his earbuds. 'Jed, too you. Wins who see let's.'

Her brother looked confused and Pippa felt sure he wasn't going to join in, but then something marvellous happened. Jed put down his Switch and shrugged. 'Will I, OK.' He took off his scarf, and turned his hoodie inside out and back to front.

Grandpa stood and grabbed his plate and mug, then took a backwards step away from the table. Pippa and Jed did the same. They walked backwards, giggling at their impromptu silliness as they turned and awkwardly dropped their dirty dishes into the sink.

'House the clean we shall?' asked Jed.

Grandpa patted him on the back. 'Jed, you thank.'

'I'll help too,' said Pippa. They pointed at her in mock horror, and she clapped her hand to her mouth. 'Too help I'll,' she corrected.

Pippa rummaged under the sink and found what she was looking for at the back of the cupboard: a roll of black bin bags. She pulled out a pair of yellow rubber gloves and a bottle of kitchen cleaner as well and handed them to Jed.

'Get started we should,' he said, taking them from her. He paused to think, realising it didn't sound quite right, then chuckled. 'Like Yoda sound I.'

Pippa shook her head. 'Wise not are you.'

Jed grinned and shoved her. 'Up shut!'

'Up shut you!'

All three of them continued the game, laughing as they worked, and before they knew it several hours had passed and they'd filled a dozen bin bags with garden waste. They went outside and emptied them on to the compost heap, then Grandpa called them over to him.

'I want you to bring the twig men down from your rooms.'

'You told us not to touch them,' Pippa reminded him.

He grunted. 'I know, but it's gone on long enough.'

Pippa started to ask a question, but he forced a smile and raised his voice. 'Be good and do as you're asked, please.'

The children shared a confused look, then did as he instructed, relieved to remove the creepy things from the house. It took several trips with the wheelbarrow, but at last they were done. Jed threw the final one on top then stamped on them, breaking apart their limbs. Thrown together in a pile they no longer resembled figures. Now they were just a heap of twigs.

'Children, done well,' said Grandpa.

Pippa grinned. They had done well. Best of all, working together had been fun.

'Them burn we shall?' she asked.

Grandpa anxiously rubbed his beard. Pippa half expected him to change his mind about getting rid of them, but he limped off to the shed.

A moment later, he returned clutching a petrol can. He poured the liquid over the twigs and gestured for them to move away. The children walked backwards, which set them off giggling again, and then Grandpa pulled a box of matches from his pocket.

A cloud drifted across the sun, casting them in shadow. At the same time the wind picked up, throwing grit into their faces. Pippa wiped her eyes then peered around the clearing, certain they were being watched. The trees shivered and shook, the wind whispering dark curses through their leaves. If someone was there, she couldn't see them. As much as she didn't like the twig men, she had a tight queasy feeling in the pit of her stomach – the kind that warned her something bad was about to happen.

'Are you sure we should do this, Grandpa?' she asked.

'No,' he answered gruffly. 'But I have to do something.'

As Grandpa opened the matches, a crow shrieked. Startled, he dropped the box. His hands trembled as he bent down and picked it up. He struck one of them and another gust of wind blew through the clearing.

Pippa was hoping the flame would go out, when he threw the match and the bonfire went up with a mighty whoosh. The three of them hurried backward and watched in silence as the flames flickered and danced. A cloud of thick grey smoke blew into Grandpa's face and he coughed violently, his shoulders shaking. Maybe it was the ferociousness of the fire, but he looked small and afraid suddenly.

Pippa chewed her fingernail and stepped closer to Jed. Neither of them smiled as they watched the twig men burn. The laughter they'd shared just moments ago had vanished, as if it too had been eaten up by the flames. Pippa was no longer proud of them doing a good job. It was just the opposite. She felt as if they'd made a terrible mistake.

6

Old Mamm stands at the edge of the clearing, watching. A circle of pine trees surrounds the house, the tallest amongst them leaning inwards as a hunter guards its prey – jealously, selfishly, hungrily. The little place didn't look so broken down the last time she came this way, but then nature will always find a way to reclaim the land. Especially here, where the woods are drenched in dark magic.

Pushing aside a heavy spruce branch, Mamm enters the garden. She's climbed the outside of a building and perched on a window ledge before, but she's never actually set foot inside a house, and they hold a strange fascination for her. With its crumbling walls and lopsided roof, this one pleases her more than the ugly red boxes that squat in rows on the edge of the forest.

While patrolling the glade and woods, she sometimes wanders the streets at night. She likes to poke her head through a window or open a letterbox and whisper through the door, sending nightmares slithering into the minds of the ones who sleep there. The children inside toss and turn and wet their beds. A few open their eyes and cry out.

After one of Mamm's little lullabies, the dark is never the same again. Their parents may smooth their hair and shush them to sleep, but the children know the truth. The night is vast and full of danger, and something unspeakable lurks in the shadows. Mamm enjoys these nightly visitations very much, but they rarely satisfy her. These days the children nearly always mistake her raspy voice for the wind in the trees and they never *see* her.

Not like the girl.

A band of mist hangs over the frosty grass. She stalks through the swirling white vapour like a ghost, then pauses when she reaches the steaming compost heap.

For now, the house is quiet.

Mamm leans against the shed and chews her knuckles, biting off a strip of ragged bark and getting a splinter in her lip. Woodlice teem inside the hessian sack of her head, making a home in the hollows of her face. Behind her left eye, a centipede wriggles, sending a ticklish shiver through her. Waiting is such delicious agony; she hasn't felt this excited in a long time. Occasionally she shifts her weight from one gnarled leg to the other, but mostly she holds still. So still that a robin lands and tugs a worm from her shoulder.

At last her patience is rewarded. She hears the girl's voice and it's like a shaft of golden sunlight filtering through the trees. The child emerges from the house, followed by a boy and an old man she's seen before. Their chatter fills her ears and lifts her spirits. She drinks in their words, greedily revels in their laughter. It reminds her of a time when there were other spriggan and she wasn't alone.

No, she mustn't remember. Loneliness is like a mushroom: it grows in dark places. She must think of the future; she must focus on the girl.

The humans enter the house and then re-emerge, each of them carrying a large black sack to the bottom of the garden. They march back and forth like a line of worker ants, and then the children return with something else in their arms.

Mamm gasps.

She knows why her masters left the twig men inside the girl's house. They won't take kindly to them being removed. No, they won't be kind at all.

The old man goes into the shed and returns holding a familiar red can. *Fire!* Her heart beats so fast, she fears it will burst. Reaching into her chest, she roots around and pulls out the flimsy sac. It pulsates in her fingers, bright with neon-green sap. Assured it's in one piece, she takes a deep breath and nestles it back in her body like she's returning a baby bird to its nest. If her masters find out she was here and did nothing . . . She *has* to stop them.

Closing her eyes, she tugs at the petrol can with her mind and wills it towards her, but the old man's grip is too strong. She calls upon the sky to darken. She calls upon the wind to scream. She calls upon the cruel-tongued crow to hurl a warning. But the humans don't listen.

Her masters fear fire as much as they hate iron, and once it gets dark they will be sure to retaliate. Only it won't just be twig men. It will be worse.

Much, much worse.

7

Pippa shivered and looked around the clearing. Wisps of pale-grey smoke writhed around the tree trunks like famished ghosts. Even though she couldn't see anyone, she knew they were there. She could feel their eyes boring into her. It was like that time when her mind had wandered off during double maths and she'd become aware of Mr Edmonds glaring at her. For some reason, she felt as if the presence watching them was angry, *livid* even.

The bonfire crackled and hissed, the heat so fierce it made her skin go tight. She'd wanted to destroy the twig men, so why did seeing their blackened remains fill her with unease? It wasn't as if they were going to drag themselves from the ashes and crawl back to her room. She imagined a charred hand poking up from the ground and her stomach tightened.

'Why don't you kids ride into town?' asked Grandpa.

He wiped his eyes with a tissue. 'Your bikes are still in the shed. Or I can give you the fare for the bus. You've worked so hard, you deserve some pocket money.'

Pippa decided she'd like to get away for a while. 'Can we call for Ollie?' she asked. Ollie was the same age as Jed and lived on the new estate that backed on to the forest. They'd met while playing in the woods a few years ago and often called for him when they visited.

Pippa nudged her brother. 'We could ask him if the den's still there.'

Jed shrugged and put his hands in his jeans pockets.

Pippa was convinced their grandfather would say no in case they went into the forest, but then Jed spoke up.

'Ollie has an Xbox. Can we go, please?'

Grandpa stared around the clearing and muttered under his breath. 'You might be safer away from here.' Before the children could ask what he meant, he ruffled Jed's hair. 'I suppose, for an hour or two . . . As long as you cycle straight there and don't go into the woods. You'll stick together, promise me now?'

'We promise,' said Jed.

Pippa nodded then dashed into the house and packed her binoculars in her rucksack. Even if she didn't get a chance to record any animals, she was excited to show them to Ollie. They quickly ate some lunch, then turned their clothes the right way round and put on their coats. Grandpa watched as they rode down the misty track. 'Don't forget, I want you home before dark!'

They cycled hard, taunting each other to go faster along the winding lanes, and by the time they arrived at Ollie's house they were both out of breath. The small red-brick building was surrounded by dozens of others that looked just the same, but parked on the drive was a large white van with the words: *Archer's Construction – no job too big or too small* painted on the side. Leaving their bikes by the front wall, the children went through the side gate and into the garden. Ollie's parents, Mr and Mrs Archer, were both outside. His dad appeared to be fixing the shed door and his mum was picking rubbish up from the lawn.

Mrs Archer straightened up and ran a hand over her long black hair, which she wore in neat cornrow braids, then waved when she saw them. A roll of sackcloth dropped from her arms and Jed retrieved it. 'Thanks, my lovely,' she said in her thick Cornish accent. 'Hold that rubbish bag open for me, would you?' Jed did as he was asked and she put the cloth inside. Resting her hands on her hips, she leaned back and appraised him. 'My, haven't you grown!' She pinched his cheek and laughed. 'Proper ansum!'

Jed's face twitched, making him squint. He shifted his weight to the other foot as if he was trying to appear smaller and Pippa shot him a pity smile. Jed didn't like people commenting on the way he looked, even if it was to tell him he was handsome.

'And, Pippa, you're . . . looking really well.'

Pippa dropped her gaze. Everyone in her class was taller than her and it didn't help that Jed was going through a growth spurt. It felt like she was being left behind. She searched the ground as if a change of subject might be hidden in the long grass. 'Did we have a storm?' she asked, looking at the plant pots, cane sticks and balls of twine everywhere.

Mrs Archer wiped her hands on her dungarees and shrugged. 'I came down this morning to find the shed door broken and the lawn a mess.' She glanced at the pine trees at the end of the garden as if something terrible might emerge from them, then turned back with a distracted smile. 'Ollie's in his room if you want to go up.'

Pippa thanked her and cautiously opened the back door. Ollie's family owned six cats who usually left the house as soon as visitors arrived, their tails held high and haughty looks on their faces, but none of them appeared, so they went inside.

The small kitchen was painted bright yellow and

filled with pot plants. A heap of washing sat on the table and the sink was overflowing with dirty dishes. Pippa wrinkled her nose. Beneath the scent of coffee and washing powder was the stink of dirty cat litter trays.

They'd just dumped their coats and bag in the hallway when Ollie's parents entered the kitchen behind them, wrinkling their noses at the smell. 'I know the cats can be moody, but it's more than that,' said Mrs Archer. 'Animals can sense things we can't.' She washed her hands in the sink and peered out of the window. 'I keep thinking about last night. The way the birds took flight like that, there must have been *hundreds* of them. It felt like a sign.'

Mr Archer chuckled good-naturedly. 'A sign of *what*, exactly?' When she didn't answer, he stepped behind her and wrapped his big muscular arms around her waist. 'You just like having something to worry about, that's what I think.' He kissed her neck and added gently, 'You and your ill omens.'

'Are you coming or what?' hissed Jed.

Pippa nodded, but didn't move. She was enjoying watching Ollie's mum and dad. They reminded her of her own parents and how they were always kissing and hugging in the house. It made her feel warm and cosy inside, and the tiniest bit homesick.

'Yowwwl!'

A black cat shot down the stairs and ran past them.

'Which one was that?' asked Jed.

Pippa shook her head. The cats all had funny names, things like Isis, Astarte and Hecate. Ollie's mum said the cats were named after goddesses – and they certainly acted with an air of self-importance.

Jed paused at the bottom of the stairs. He placed a protective hand on Pippa's arm and a warm glow of gratitude filled her chest. On the landing were two stern-faced Siamese. Sitting perfectly still, they looked like statues that might come alive and ask you a riddle before letting you pass. As he approached them they hissed and jumped up his legs. 'Quick, Newt! Run!'

Pushing past him, she made a dash for Ollie's door and knocked three times then waited and gave it another quick three raps. It was a code they'd made up while playing in the woods once, so they knew it was safe to allow one another into the den.

Ollie opened the door and grinned. Unlike Jed, who was tall and thin, he seemed to have grown outwards over the past few months. With his round glasses and short curly black hair, he made Pippa think of a sleepy mole.

'Who's there?' he asked.

Pippa frowned. 'Ollie?'

'Hey, Newt! I didn't see you down there!'

Pippa made a show of folding her arms. She tried to be angry, but Ollie was so lovable and silly it was hard to be mad at him. He pulled her into a bear hug and lifted her feet off the floor. 'I've missed you,' he laughed.

'Erm, could someone help me, please?' shouted Jed, trying to shake off a cat that had clambered on to his head.

Ollie pulled off the feline assassin. 'That's enough now, Kali!' The cat continued its attack and he grappled with its twisting body. 'I don't know what's got into them. They've gone really weird and won't leave the house.'

'None of them?' asked Pippa, thinking that explained the smell in the kitchen.

Ollie turned and ran into his room, landing with a customary belly flop on to his bed. The place was even messier than usual. The large black shelving unit that contained his TV and Xbox was covered with half-eaten sandwiches, empty Pot Noodles and cans of Coke. A slimy brown banana skin hung from one of the shelves, seemingly having missed its trajectory on the way to the bin.

Jed jumped on to the bed next to their friend. Folding his long legs beneath him, he flicked his fringe and pointed at the image on the TV. 'Is that the new FIFA?'

'Yeah, bro. It's the best. Do you have it?'

Jed picked up a controller. 'Nah, but I've heard it's awesome.'

The sound of football cheers filled the room and Pippa's heart sank. She knew Jed would want to play Xbox, but she was hoping the three of them could have done something else first. Maybe she should say something. Not wanting to seem a killjoy, she decided to keep quiet. Hopefully they'd play for a while and then ask her what *she* wanted to do.

She tiptoed across the minefield of dirty pants and socks, then took a seat at Ollie's desk under the window. As she gazed at the slate-grey clouds, she found herself wishing she'd seen the birds take flight last night. Something must have disturbed them, she supposed, though how that could be a sign of anything she didn't know.

And then a thought occurred to her. Yesterday, her dad had accused Grandpa of being superstitious. If Grandpa believed in ill omens like Mrs Archer, maybe that's why he put the twig men in the house. But if that was the case, why burn them?

'Ollie, is it OK if I use your laptop?' she asked.

He answered without taking his eyes from the

screen. 'Sure. You're not looking up pictures of cute boys, are you?'

'How did you guess?'

She opened the search bar and typed *superstitions twig men*. The usual stuff about black cats and not walking under ladders came up, but nothing to explain why anyone would fill their house with creepy twig figures. She added *Cornwall* and *West Penwith* and this time there were lots of pages. Apparently the area had the highest concentration of ancient sites in Europe – over seven hundred of them, some more than four thousand years old.

She looked outside at the swirling white fog and rubbed her arms. It was strange to think of there being so many ancient places nearby. Turning back to the screen, she clicked a link that caught her interest. By the time she'd finished reading, a chill had crept over her skin that had nothing to do with the weather.

Hidden folk and otherworldly beings of West Cornwall

One commonly held belief is that ancient sites such as hill forts, stone circles and barrows are the home of the hidden folk – invisible winged creatures that are part human and part animal (*see Distant Relations of Faeries*). Some are said to be kindly beings that protect nature and do no harm to people, while others delight in playing cruel tricks on humans. Stray on to their land or steal their treasure and they may turn your milk sour, cause your crops to fail or bring illness to your family. According to folklore they can be scared away with iron or fire. Wearing one's clothes inside out is also believed to keep them at bay.

Grandpa had been wearing his jumper inside out when they arrived yesterday, and he still hadn't put it straight. Had he invented the backwards game so they would turn their clothes inside out too?

'Newt, why don't you have a go?'

Pippa jumped at the sound of Jed's voice. She turned and Ollie was crawling over the bed towards her, pointing at the laptop. 'She's not looking at boys. She's looking at pictures of faeries!'

'Faeries?' echoed Jed incredulously.

Pippa folded her arms. 'They're called hidden folk.' The boys laughed and she couldn't have felt more embarrassed if she *had* been looking at cute boys. 'So what if I am?' she snapped. 'I don't make fun of you for jabbing buttons all day.'

Jed's face flushed pink. He shot an awkward glance at Ollie then clenched his jaw and smiled uneasily at his sister. 'Here,' he said, holding out his Xbox controller to her. 'If you don't want to play FIFA, you can always play Fortnite. I'll show you how it works. Come on, it'll be fun.'

'No, it won't! Gaming is all you ever do and it's boring!'

It came out harsher than she intended and she wished she could have taken it back, even before she saw the hurt look on her brother's face.

'What do you know?' asked Jed, his cheek twitching. 'You're just a kid.' He turned back to the screen and resumed the game, muttering, 'Climbing trees is boring. *You're* boring.'

Pippa looked at Ollie but he was staring at the controller in his hands, refusing to meet her gaze. Of course the boys were going to stick together. Suddenly she felt the way she did in school: the annoying little sister that no one wants around. Cheeks burning, she marched to the door. 'Fine, I'll go.'

Pippa left the room and paused on the landing. She and Jed had been getting on so well this morning and now it was ruined. She hoped he might follow her, but he didn't. Swallowing her disappointment, she ran down the stairs. She wasn't going to stick around and be ignored. She knew when she wasn't wanted.

8

Mamm watches the children ride up the misty lane. If they stray into the forest they could be in danger – and not just from her.

She turns away, confused by the way she feels. Lodged within her is a kernel of hate; like a sour little apple that never ripens or rots, it's there each time she re-forms. She has no control over the way she feels; anger is simply a part of her. She feels an urge to hurt the children, yet there's something about the girl that stops her. It's not just that she wants the child to give up her name. Mamm feels drawn to her in a way she can't explain.

All the times she's crouched on children's windowsills and watched them sleep . . . why did *this* girl see her?

All of a sudden, she realises. The child may live in a house, but she spends most of her time outdoors. She hugs the trees and talks with the birds and insects as if they're old friends. Like Mamm, the girl belongs to the forest. Watching the child play had made her feel a little less alone.

'A word with you, spriggan.'

Mamm spins round, startled by the unexpected voice. A bedraggled crow hops along the shed roof, its beady black eyes glinting with menace. She's used to the birds constantly cawing, but she's never heard one speak. Animals don't talk, not unless . . . Her body stiffens with realisation. It's the crow she called upon to warn the humans. Only it's not a bird, but a watcher – a creature of magic made by her masters. How did she not notice before? *Stupid Mamm!* If she hadn't drawn its attention, it might not have seen what the old man was burning. The bird will have flown straight to the glade and informed her masters.

The crow dips its head. 'You, spriggan, are summoned to *caw* the elders.'

Her knees go weak. She nods and asks quietly, 'When?'

The crow hops gleefully from foot to foot. 'Now!' it caws harshly. 'Now! Now!'

She waits until the bird flaps away, then collapses against the shed and covers her face with her hands. The seven elders make and uphold the laws, ruling over the rest of her masters. They'll want to know why she didn't deal with the girl when she touched the stone in summer. If she'd done her job properly, the child would never have returned to the forest. They'll say she's failed them.

Mamm wrings her gnarled hands. She's seen others of her kind dragged before the elders and it never ended well. If she's no longer able to serve her purpose, they'll send her to ground for good. She's endured so much, lost all those she's ever loved, fallen apart and remade herself so many times. Some days she gets so lonely it feels like a weight is crushing her chest. She can't remember the last time she shared a kind word or felt the comforting touch of another. Could this really be the end?

Shush now, Mamm. Get a hold of yourself. You've survived worse than this.

Taking a steadying breath, she smooths the side of her head as if she means to keep it. A scrap of mouldy sackcloth falls away, leaving a gaping hole in her temple. The cold slices into her like steel wire, making her wince. She knows she's growing weaker, but her body doesn't usually disintegrate until she's in the earth. Perhaps her masters have already decided this will be her last incarnation? No. If that were the case they wouldn't have called her to stand trial.

Mamm's legs feel heavy as they carry her into the glade. Where she walks, tiny red-and-white-spotted mushrooms spring up. Their bright spongy caps fill her empty footprints, forming a crimson trail in the long grass. Animals gather at the edge of the clearing: squirrels, foxes, rabbits, deer. A dozen tiny frogs watch as she goes by, blinking like uncertain jury members. Hundreds of birds line the trees. More and more of them come, until the bare branches are laden with their brooding dark shapes. The wind has dropped and the world holds its misty breath. Even the crows are silent for once.

It's not safe for the animals to be here, so near to her masters' lair, but they cannot help themselves. The glade's ancient magic draws all beings close and its energy is stronger than ever today, the day the elders hold council. Though she knows the animals have no choice, Mamm doesn't like the feeling of being surrounded by a crowd. She doesn't like the feeling of being watched.

In the centre of the clearing is the stone: a large, flat granite slab resting on top of two boulders. Slime-swollen slugs and furry wet lichen criss-cross its surface, glistening darkly in the pale, foggy light. A chill breeze rips the leaves from the trees and they scatter down in a furious whirlwind. She steps closer,

her body trembling. Soft murmuring fills the hollow –
the sound of a hundred whispering voices. The noise
grows louder, the voices becoming increasingly
urgent, until Mamm's head rings with the magic of
her masters.

Before her, the hole throbs with blackness, seeming
to grow bigger and darker, welcoming her like open
jaws. She rests a hand on top of the granite and lichen
creeps up her fingers and covers her wrist like a bruise.
The stone's coldness burrows into her, spreading into
her aching joints, invading her soft parts. A tang of
sour apple floods her mouth as the kernel of anger
within her grows. She is borne from the same hateful
magic as her masters, bonded to them by thorn and
root, pain and bone. They command and she obeys.

Not yet. Just a little while longer, please . . .

She closes her eyes and feels the gentle rays of the
sun on her face, imprinting the warmth on to her body
and her memory. Inhaling deeply, she fills herself with
the musty scents of the forest. Then she opens her
eyes and looks into the darkness. Her heart falters.
She doesn't want to enter the ground, yet go into the
ground she must.

9

Pippa was about to grab her coat and bag from the hallway when she saw Ollie's mum drying up at the kitchen sink. Only she wasn't actually moving her hands. She was staring out of the window with a tense look on her face, a tea towel in one hand and a plate in the other. Water dripped from it, making a puddle on the draining board. Pippa decided she wouldn't go home just yet after all. She doubted Mrs Archer believed in hidden folk, but she might know something about the superstitions of the area. Perhaps she knew about the twig men.

'Hi,' said Pippa.

Mrs Archer spun round and the plate fell to the floor, smashing to pieces.

'I'm sorry, I didn't mean to . . .'

'Don't worry,' said Mrs Archer, bending down. 'These things happen.'

Feeling awkward, Pippa moved out of the way and

stood by the window. The fog was thicker now. It hung over the garden like a heavy grey blanket, smothering the grass and obscuring the dark outline of the shed. She could barely see the trees at the end of the garden.

'What was there?' she asked.

'Sorry?' said Mrs Archer, dropping the broken crockery into the bin.

'You were looking at something outside.'

'Was I? I suppose I was thinking about the birds last night. Did you see them?'

Pippa shook her head.

'Hundreds of them flew up at once; it was quite something.' She peered outside and her voice sounded small and far away. 'You know, I haven't seen a single one today.'

Pippa checked the grey slab of sky and found it empty. She thought about the crow that had screamed, making Grandpa drop the matches. Come to think of it, she hadn't seen or heard another bird since then. Perhaps they were hiding in the trees. She stepped into the hallway and took her binoculars from her bag. 'You could use these if you like?'

Mrs Archer took them and held them to her eyes. 'Wow! The definition is amazing. You can really see things in detail, can't you? Shame it's so foggy.'

Pippa's chest warmed with pride. 'They have an infrared setting so you can use them at night. They can record video too.'

'Can they really?' said Mrs Archer, continuing to scan the garden and pausing every now and then to peer at something she'd seen. It was nice that an adult was taking an interest, but Pippa was soon impatient for her to give them back.

'Can you see any birds?' she asked.

'I'm afraid not,' replied Mrs Archer, handing the binoculars to her.

Pippa fiddled with a tiny dial on the side of them. 'I was wondering, why's it an ill omen to see lots of birds?' Ollie's mum stiffened and Pippa added in a rush, 'Sorry, I didn't mean to eavesdrop. Only I'm interested in the superstitions of the area. It's for a school project I'm doing.'

'I see,' said Mrs Archer. 'What would you like to know?'

Pippa smiled with relief. Saying that you were doing a project for school always seemed to go down well with grown-ups. She didn't want to give the impression she believed in otherworldly beings, or that Grandpa might. She thought for a moment then asked, 'Why would someone hang life-size twig men in their house?'

'Sorry, that's a new one on me. I've heard of corn dollies, but not twig men.'

'What about hidden folk?'

Mrs Archer's face tightened. Lowering her gaze, she picked up the tea towel and hurriedly started to dry the breakfast things. 'What about them?'

'Is it true they live at ancient stone sites?'

'I believe so, yes.'

'I know they don't really exist, but do some people believe in them? I read they can play tricks on humans and wearing your clothes inside out is meant to keep them away.'

Ollie's mum clutched the tea towel and glanced around the kitchen as if something sinister was hiding in one of the cupboards. The room appeared normal to Pippa, yet for some reason she felt oddly uneasy, as if she'd said something wrong.

Mrs Archer lowered her voice to a whisper. 'Some things are best not spoken about. It can invite things that . . . well, that aren't welcome.' She started to say something else, then stopped and stared at the hallway as if she'd seen something.

Pippa looked over her shoulder. There was no one there and nothing to see apart from a horseshoe hanging above the open door. Ollie's mum might be superstitious, but talking about something that didn't exist was hardly going to invite it into your house. She must have meant something else.

Pippa was about to ask, when Ollie and Jed came charging down the stairs, laughing and nudging one another. They entered the room and Mrs Archer smiled as if she was glad of the distraction. 'Can I get you kids a snack?' She turned and began rummaging through a cupboard. 'I think there are some chocolate muffins left.'

'Great, I'm starving,' said Ollie.

Pippa noticed him looking at her binoculars and saw an opportunity to smooth things over between them. 'I was just showing these to your mum. I got them for my birthday so I can record nocturnal animals.' Jed sighed, seemingly bored of hearing about it. She faltered but then continued. 'We could go outside and try them out if you like?'

'Nah,' said Ollie. 'I'm happy gaming, thanks.'

Pippa shrugged and tried not to look as disappointed as she felt. The children pulled out some chairs and Mrs Archer lifted the washing from the table. Seeming to notice the tension between them, she leaned forward and whispered to Ollie, 'Sometimes you have to do what your friends want. Come on, there must be something you can all play together.' When he didn't answer, she added brightly, 'I know, how about a game of Twister!'

The children shared a pained look. They might disagree about what they wanted to do, but none of them wanted to crawl around on the floor and get their limbs tangled up in knots.

Ollie grabbed the binoculars and pushed his glasses up his nose. 'My cousin Taylor has some like this. She uses them to go ghost hunting in abandoned buildings.'

Pippa sat up a little straighter. 'She uses them at night?'

'Yeah. She showed me the footage she captured at this disused abattoir once. She reckons it was a ghost, but I think it was just her shadow.'

'Could have been a ghost pig,' said Jed. He grunt-snorted, adding 'oink oink' for good measure, and both boys laughed and shook their heads.

Pippa presumed it was some in-joke between them, but didn't want to ask in case they only laughed more. She didn't have any feelings about ghosts one way or the other. What interested her was that Ollie's cousin used the binoculars at night, which meant she must know how to use the infrared setting. 'Do you think Taylor would show me how they work?' she asked.

Ollie frowned in puzzlement and Jed butted in. 'Newt lost the instructions.'

Pippa glared at Jed. He made it sound like she was careless, but it wasn't like that. Mum had accidentally put them through the shredder with a pile of paperwork. They'd searched for the instructions online, but hadn't been able to find anything. 'It wasn't my fault. Mum chucked them,' she explained.

Ollie nodded sympathetically, as if he knew the trauma of having a parent who tidied his belongings into the bin. 'Taylor works in the bookshop in town. I'm meant to be helping her tomorrow. I'll ask if she still has the instructions for hers. Maybe she can photocopy them.'

'Thanks, that would be great,' said Pippa.

Mrs Archer put a plate of muffins on the table. The children began to eat and soon they were chatting about last summer.

'Is the den we built still there?' asked Pippa.

Ollie demolished a muffin in two quick bites then licked his fingers. 'Yeah, it's lost part of the back wall, but it's still standing.'

'We could fix it up and play zombies in the fog,' suggested Pippa.

Jed yawned and cut his muffin into quarters.

'Could be fun,' said Ollie. 'Bagsy I get to be zombie first!' He glanced at Jed, who still hadn't raised his eyes from the table. 'Or we can stay inside if you're tired?'

'I'm not tired,' said Jed defensively.

'He's just in energy-saving mode,' said Pippa. 'At a cellular level he's actually really busy.'

Jed gave her a tiny smile and she was pleased he seemed amused and not angry with her for once. Feeling better than she had in a while, she finished her muffin then pushed back her chair. She knew they weren't meant to go into the forest, but the den was so close it was practically at the bottom of Ollie's garden. Once they were outside, Jed would remember the fun they'd had in summer and hopefully want to play with her again.

The children had just grabbed their coats and were heading to the back door when Mrs Archer stopped them. 'Sorry, guys, but maybe you should think about getting back. This fog isn't lifting. If it gets much worse, you won't be able to see to ride home.'

Jed looked at his feet. 'We told Grandpa we'd only be an hour or two.'

Pippa didn't want to leave, not when they were finally about to go out and have fun. But she didn't want Grandpa to worry about them. 'Thanks for the muffins,' she said glumly.

Mrs Archer patted her on the back. 'You're welcome. It's always nice to see you.'

The boys fist-bumped and Ollie gave Pippa a hug,

which cheered her up a bit. Before she knew it, they were walking around the side of the house and promising to meet up again soon. Mrs Archer followed them out and watched as they got on to their bikes. 'Take care on the roads now.' She glanced up the misty lane then gave them a worried look. It seemed to Pippa she was anxious about more than just the fog.

10

The light was fading from the sky by the time the children returned. They hadn't said much during the ride back and Pippa could sense Jed's mood worsening as they put their bikes in the shed.

'It won't be dark for another hour. We could play in the garden for a bit,' she suggested.

Before Jed could answer, Grandpa appeared at the front door and ushered them inside. 'I was starting to worry about you,' he grumbled. He bolted the door behind them and then followed the children into the kitchen. Pippa was relieved to see it still looking normal: the floor no longer covered with leaves and no twig men hanging in the window. At the same time, the room felt bare and empty without them.

While the children washed their hands and sat down, Grandpa took a casserole from the oven. Pippa fought the urge to groan. He'd made them beef stew and dumplings and must have forgotten that she didn't like it. Still, it was nice of him to cook. Dad once told her he'd stopped eating properly after Grandma died, choosing to live off sandwiches and tinned fruit.

Pippa had been a baby when Grandma passed away, so she didn't remember her. She'd seen photos though, and sometimes Grandpa would tell stories about her and how she'd been a chef in a fancy hotel in London. He said she had so much goodness in her that she couldn't contain it all inside. It had to go somewhere, so it found its way into the food she made. When she died, he said his taste-buds shrivelled up and nothing tasted good again.

Pippa lifted her fork. 'Thanks, Grandpa. It looks great.'

He sat on the chair to her right and absent-mindedly rubbed his leg.

'How's your knee?' she asked.

'Pardon?'

'Your knee,' she shouted.

His eyes flicked to the door and he mumbled something under his breath. Pippa couldn't understand it. He'd seemed like his old self this morning – inventing silly games and making them laugh. His jumper was still on inside out. Could he have kept it that way for a reason? She looked at Jed,

78

wishing she could talk to him about it, but he was wearing his earbuds and playing a game. At least he wouldn't hear what she was about to say.

'I had a chat with Ollie's mum today. She was telling me about the superstitions of the area. We talked about hidden folk and how . . .'

Grandpa got up from the table, his dinner untouched. She heard him shuffle to the front door and rattle the bolt as if checking it was locked. Then he returned and made sure the window latches were fixed. Perhaps he was worried about burglars.

'Are you OK, Grandpa?'

'What?'

Pippa shook her head. This was hopeless. Maybe she should get a notepad and pen and write things down for him.

They ate in silence for a while then Grandpa yanked out one of Jed's earbuds. 'Once you've finished eating, I want you both to go up to your rooms and read or play your games until bedtime.'

Jed frowned. 'Why?'

'Just do as you're told,' snapped Grandpa. He rubbed his temples as if he had a headache, then softened his voice. 'The rodents I told you about have been in the house again. I've blocked up all the holes, but if they come back I'll need to catch them.'

Pippa thought about the scratching noise in her room this morning and the mess they'd made. Maybe that's all it was – Grandpa was upset about rats being in the house.

'Me and Jed can help,' she offered.

'No!' said Grandpa. 'Under no circumstances are you to come downstairs.'

Jed snorted and shoved back his chair. 'You don't want us here, I get it! I don't want to be here either!' This time he didn't wait for Pippa to leave the room with him. He dumped his dirty plate in the sink and charged upstairs. A moment later she heard his door slam.

Grandpa gestured for Pippa to follow Jed, then grunted when she showed no sign of moving.

'Are you sure it's just rats you're worried about, Grandpa?' He looked at her blankly, so she got up from the table and hugged him. 'OK. Night then.'

'You know I love you, don't you?' he whispered, pulling her close and patting her hair. Pippa tightened her arms around his neck, enjoying the feel of his soft shirt against her cheek and the familiar scent of soap and wood smoke. She wanted so much to talk to him, not just about the twig men, but about how Jed had been so different with her lately and how he was always arguing with their parents at home. A lump came to her throat and she wished again that Grandpa's hearing wasn't so bad.

Pulling away, he looked at her tenderly. 'Make sure you stay in your room, whatever you hear.' She nodded, even though it seemed silly to be worried about a few rats. 'Good girl. Off you go now.'

Pippa gave him another big squeeze then trudged up the stairs. Pausing on the landing, she wondered whether to knock on Jed's door and tell him what she'd read at Ollie's house. It was hard to imagine anyone could believe in hidden folk, but if Grandpa did it might explain a few things. Jed knew more than her when it came to grown-ups. A while ago he'd explained that Dad was moody with them because he was worried about the restaurant losing money, and when Pippa had got into trouble at school once, he'd told her how teachers don't really want an answer when they say *What have you got to say for yourself?*

If only she could talk things through with him, maybe Grandpa's odd behaviour would make sense. The sound of gunfire came from inside his room and she hung her head. Even if she apologised for saying Xbox was boring, she doubted it would make a difference. Now he'd fallen out with Grandpa, he'd be in an even worse mood.

Pippa glanced at Jed's door one final time, a familiar knot of worry in her chest, and then turned away. She couldn't remember the last time she'd felt this lonely.

Her bedroom was cold and her things were still a mess from this morning. She tidied up and was about to start reading a book on fungi when a pale shape swooped by the window: a barn owl perhaps? She grabbed her binoculars and scanned the sky. She knew they hunted at night and ate shrews and mice, swallowing their prey whole and coughing up the bits of fur and bone as pellets. A buzz of excitement rose inside her. Imagine if she recorded one catching a mouse!

The buttery moon hung low in the sky, its round face gleaming like an invitation. Even if she couldn't get the infrared setting to work on her binoculars, there should be enough light to capture a bird in flight. Grandpa had told them not to enter the forest or Whispering Hollow, but he hadn't said anything about the garden. She wouldn't be gone long.

Pippa put on her coat then slung her binoculars around her neck and opened the window. Leaning out, she felt to her right. Her fingers touched leafy wet ivy then closed around something hard: a drainpipe. She'd never climbed it before as Grandpa had never minded her playing out after dark, but she'd scrambled down the one at home lots of times.

Pulling herself up on to the windowsill, she turned her body and found a foothold in the crumbling brickwork. Cold white vapour swirled around her jeans as she climbed down, and for a moment she felt as if she was moving through clouds. Few things were more thrilling than venturing into the night, and every nerve ending in her body tingled.

Seconds later, she was on the ground and hurrying away from the house. The moon cast an eerie glow over everything, throwing jagged shards of black across the grass and forming monstrous shapes from the bushes. She loved how the darkness could do that: make the ordinary world feel strange and new.

She often explored the garden at home after dark, but it was nothing like this. Here the crisp night air was alive with the scent of pine and the rich smells of the earth. The housing estate on the edge of the forest didn't give off the same ghastly yellow glow as the streetlights in the city, and there were no trains rumbling nearby or planes flying overhead. The sky was a vast dome streaked with rivers of stars, so bright she could almost touch them.

Moving quickly, she stayed in the shadows and skirted around the edge of the garden. Her pulse quickened as she passed the ashen remains of the bonfire. Not wanting to think about the twig men, she fixed her gaze ahead. Before her stood the splintered oak tree, its blackened trunk emerging from the mist like a finger accusing the sky. She knew every foothold on its gnarled body and would have loved to climb it, but there was something she wanted more.

The thought of going into Whispering Hollow – of entering somewhere forbidden – always excited her, and tonight the pull of the place was irresistible. She found her feet carried her there in the strange way of a dream, and she could no more have turned back than flapped her arms and flown. She looked through the binoculars as she walked and had almost reached the line of laurel bushes when something swooped overhead. She pressed the record button and a tiny red dot appeared in the darkness, pulsing in time with her heart.

A shadow sped over the ground, but when she looked up there was nothing there. Perhaps it had flown into the glade? She pictured a majestic owl gliding over the stone with its wings outstretched. It would be the perfect shot. She *had* to get it.

She stepped towards the bushes then stopped. For some reason, Grandpa seemed to think it was dangerous. Perhaps he knew something she didn't? She had decided to go back when a stab of desire pierced her heart. She *really* wanted to see the stone. And it wasn't like she hadn't entered the glade before. In summer, she'd touched the stone and even peeked into the hole beneath it. Grandpa hadn't found out then, and nothing bad had happened.

Low whispering filled the air. It was more than just the wind in the trees; she could almost make out words. The sound of voices swirled around her, coming from every side.

'*Pi-ppaaa. Pi-ppaaa.*'

Someone or something was calling her name, drawing her forward.

She tried to turn back, but she couldn't. Her body moved by itself, her limbs willed by an unseen force. She pushed through the leafy branches and gasped. The stone shone like a jewel, illuminated by a single shaft of moonlight. It was even more beautiful than she imagined. It was magical.

At her feet, a line of green frogs croaked and jumped. Dozens of slugs and snails made their way across the ground, moving faster than seemed possible. She gazed at them, unable to comprehend what she was seeing. More animals scampered past her through the long grass: a family of sleek brown voles, followed by several squirrels and a train of shuffling spiky hedgehogs. All of them were heading towards the stone. Before she could wonder what it might mean, something rustled in the bushes.

Shaking her head as if rousing herself from a daydream, she checked the binoculars were still recording and lifted them to her eyes. Perhaps a fox or badger was about to enter the clearing? She fiddled with the dial and the grainy black and white image came into focus.

Pippa turned cold. There was something crouched at the edge of the glade, but it wasn't an animal. The creature had the skinny white limbs of a child, but something about its proportions made her shudder. They were . . . wrong somehow. It came to the height of her knee, yet it looked like a grown person. The thing turned its head and through a lank curtain of hair she caught a glimpse of a feral face and a flash of sharp teeth. Scrawny arms, as pale as bone, ended in black-clawed fingers. Within its grasp struggled a mouse.

Pippa swallowed, her mouth suddenly dry. She lowered the binoculars with shaking hands then blinked. There was nothing there. When she looked through them again the creature reappeared. It resembled an old man, but it had long whiskers, hairy pointed ears and eyes on either side of its head, like a rabbit. Pressing the zoom button, she watched as it opened its mouth to reveal a row of needle-sharp teeth. It snapped the rodent's neck and greedily gulped at the air, seeming to drink something she couldn't see. When it was done, it wiped its lips with the back of its hand and threw the limp-bodied mouse into the grass.

Pippa's breath came hard and fast. She wanted to run, but some strange fascination kept her rooted to the spot. What *was* that thing? And why was she only able to see it through the binoculars? She stumbled back, her mind reeling.

Snap.

She'd stepped on a twig.

The creature swivelled its head towards her, its eyes glowing white in the darkness. A pair of huge leathery wings unfurled from its back and furiously beat the air. It shrieked, its face twisted with hatred, and she knew then that it meant to hurt her.

11

Mamm sits on the grass and lowers herself into the hole like a swimmer easing their body into an ice-cold lake. The drop is further than she remembers and she lands awkwardly, twisting her knee. *Crack.* A pine cone splits from her leg and bounces away across the ground. Gasping in pain, she gets on all fours and desperately scrabbles around in the leaves and dirt.

Her eyes haven't adjusted to the red gloom surrounding her and she blinks and stares. *Where is the blasted thing? Hurry, Mamm, you can't let them see you like this!* Her masters delight in the suffering of others and feast on fear like a dog sucks on marrow. If they sense she's weak, it will only sharpen their appetite. At last, her fingers close around something hard. 'Aha, got you!' Lodging the pine cone back where it belongs, she scrambles to her feet.

The tunnel is long and airless, the roof low and riddled with dangling tree roots. A vivid crimson glow emanates from the other end, so that the walls appear drenched in blood. Piles of dead leaves and fragments of white bone litter the ground. As she walks, something crunches under her foot, the skull of a long-dead animal, its life sucked from its body.

Mamm has heard of other groups of masters who live above ground and protect the natural world, dwelling in the rivers, forests and valleys, who do no harm to humans. Why her masters choose to live like this makes no sense to her. It doesn't seem right to spend your days in darkness and only venture into the world at night. The ground is a place where things fester and rot, where things go to die.

Years ago, Mamm made a home with her kind in the woods. They laughed and chased one another through the trees and splashed in the stream. At night, they curled up together under the velvet-black sky and slept under swathes of twinkling diamonds. They woke each morning covered with green ooze and thaw, the pine-bright air crystal sharp in their lungs.

Life was perfect . . . until a human would encroach on the glade. Then the angry dark magic of their masters would fill them with fury and they'd have no choice but to harm the trespassers. The threat of being sent to ground was always present. Spriggan are never free – however much they yearn to be.

Mamm knows to tend the tiny flame within her and does her best to keep it burning with tender thoughts and memories, even in her darkest moments. But as she walks towards the intense red glow before her, the happiness she once cherished feels so far away.

Movement flickers at the edge of her vision. The compacted soil heaves and shifts, the tree roots twisting and turning like writhing snakes. Streams of dirt pour down and patter over her shoulders as dozens of faces push their way out of the walls then quickly disappear again. The crude shapes ripple along the tunnel like a shadow following her every step. Even without turning her head, she knows her masters are close. It reeks of them, the stench of bad blood and bitterness foul on the air.

The thought of entering the courtroom makes her legs go weak. Her masters show no mercy, not even to their own kind. Mamm has seen them drag their young to the stone and put them to death in the most gruesome of ways simply for daring to question their leaders.

The elders.

Hope shrinks inside her. She's almost there. They'll be waiting for her.

12

Pippa turned and ran back through the bushes. Branches tore at her coat and scratched her face. She glanced over her shoulder and lifted the binoculars. The creature was following her, its wings outstretched. Stifling a sob, she charged across the lawn. The sound of beating wings filled the air. Forcing her legs to move faster, she reached the house then grabbed the drainpipe and began to climb.

She'd almost reached the top, when something clawed her leg. Her palms were sweaty and she slipped on the window ledge and teetered, nearly losing her balance, her fingers just managing to grip the thick vines of ivy. Shaking with panic, she jumped through the window and landed on the carpet with a thud.

She couldn't shout for Grandpa. He'd be so angry with her. Getting to her feet, she rushed on to the landing and frantically rapped on her brother's door.

'Jed!'

The sound of explosions came from inside. She was about to knock again, when he opened the door.

'What?'

'Please, you have to see this.'

She held out the binoculars and Jed sighed. 'I'm in the middle of a game.'

'Just look, would you!'

Barging past him, Pippa sat on his bed and pressed the rewind button. The image on the screen began to play and she watched the flickering footage, waiting for the glade and the creature to appear. Only it didn't. It was a video of their garden at home.

'It's not there!' she cried.

'What's not there?'

'It was like a really small person but it had wings and glowing white eyes. It was holding this mouse and . . . It chased me, I swear!'

'Is this a joke?' asked Jed.

She rushed to the window and a cloud drifted across the moon, sending shadowy fingers creeping across the lawn. The creature *couldn't* have been real. Yet she'd seen it.

'I'm telling the truth, Jed. It was scary.'

He gave a tiny laugh. '*You*, scared?'

Pippa felt herself tense. Jed often made comments about how brave she was, and while she liked to think he was proud of her, sometimes it felt like a criticism. Before she'd started high school, she'd told him she was nervous the other kids wouldn't like her. Instead of reassuring her, he'd snapped, 'You're outgoing and sporty; of course you'll be popular.' As it happened she'd made friends quickly, but it felt like because she wasn't afraid of other things – spiders, or heights, or the dark – then she wasn't allowed to be fearful about anything.

Jed stood by her side and wiped the condensation from the glass. 'Maybe it was a fox.'

'It had wings.'

'An owl then.'

She searched for the file again, but it wasn't there. Why hadn't it recorded? And why had she only been able to see the creature when she was looking through the binoculars? It didn't make sense.

'Perhaps it was a trick of the light,' he offered. 'The moon could have created a glare on the lens.' When she didn't answer, he asked, 'How small was it?'

She gestured to her knee.

'So about half a metre and it looked like a person but had wings?'

'Yes.'

Jed smirked. 'When we were at Ollie's house, what were you looking at online?'

Pippa's face flushed. 'I *didn't* imagine it! I think it might have been one of the hidden folk.'

Jed gave her a look that said he was worried about her. 'If it makes you feel any better, we'll go out there now and search for it if you want.'

She shook her head. The thought of seeing the creature again sent a slither of fear down her spine.

'So what *do* you want to do?' he asked.

Pippa fiddled with the strap of her binoculars. She didn't want Grandpa to know she'd disobeyed him. But what if he'd seen the creature too? He was obviously afraid of something. She had to tell him, but the thought of going downstairs and facing his anger was more than she could bear. What she really wanted was to be at home, safe in bed.

'Nothing,' she said at last. 'Not tonight anyway.' Jed gave her a confused frown and she forced a smile. 'Sorry for interrupting your game.'

With that, she pulled his door closed and went to her room. There were so many thoughts whirling in her head that she felt dizzy with them. She shut the window then closed the curtains and changed into her pyjamas. As she got into bed, she wished Mum was there to give her a hug. There was no phone signal and the landline wasn't working, so she couldn't call and ask her parents to collect them. And what would happen to Grandpa? They couldn't go back to London and leave him here, not with that thing outside.

As Pippa pulled the covers up, a thought came to her. The first time she'd used the binoculars at night she'd filmed a fox in their garden at home. When she'd searched for the infrared file, nothing had come up at first. She'd fiddled around with the settings, not knowing what she was doing, and it had suddenly appeared. Maybe she *had* recorded the creature and just needed to figure out how to retrieve it.

Pippa jumped out of bed and grabbed the binoculars. She tried various settings, jabbing the buttons in different orders, but couldn't get it to work. Tired and defeated, she switched off the light and climbed back under the covers. When she closed her eyes, she didn't drift into a welcome sleep; instead she saw the illuminated screen of her binoculars imprinted on her brain. Clenching her fists in frustration, she lay on her back and stared into the darkness. Eventually sleep took her . . . straight into a nightmare.

13

As Mamm continues down the tunnel, a maelstrom of moths flutters about her, their shabby grey wings brushing her face and hands. She peers at one and recoils; in place of an insect's body is a tiny human skeleton. She's never liked the magical creations of her masters, despite being one herself. At least the ones above ground look as if they belong to the natural world. Not like down here, where all kinds of twisted monstrosities infest the air and crawl the walls.

She swats the peculiar things away then looks around in case anyone saw. Her masters have the ability to turn invisible; she could be alone or she could be surrounded by them. Unsure if she's being watched, she hurries on down the tunnel. Like a rabbit's warren, there are endless openings leading off to further chambers and passageways.

A thin wail slices the air.

Glancing into a chamber to her left, she sees a master kneeling on the ground, his head bowed. Five others stand around him. They take it in turns to strike him, laughing as they slash his face with their claws. Repulsed, she quickens her pace. She doesn't know why her masters hurt their own kind, but then so many of their ways are strange to her, like why they make mischief in the homes of humans yet despise being seen by them. She supposes that's why they created a race of bodyguards to defend their realm against trespassers. Unlike them, spriggans don't fear being seen by humans. They yearn for it.

Without meaning to, she thinks of her brother, Spring Foot. His mossy beard, the way cuckoo-spit dribbled down his chin when he laughed, the splay of his bushy green feet. She doesn't know how many seasons have passed since his trial, but she recalls their slow and solemn march to stand before the elders that day.

It's hard to believe she's taking the same route now; it looks so different. Back then, there were twenty spriggan living above ground and they'd faced the elders together. Their masters had lined the grand hallways in their hundreds, all of them leering and shouting. Her brother had squeezed her hand, insisting he'd been careful and no one knew his secret.

Spring Foot said there was a boy who lived in the forest that wasn't afraid like the others. He said there was a real connection between them. Once the boy told him his name the two of them would be bonded, and their masters would no longer have a hold over him.

Mamm had heard of such things, everyone had – when a human gives you their name it acts as a magical contract, cutting the ties between spriggan and master. Only you can't ask; they must give it freely. She desperately hoped her brother was right, but it wasn't to be.

A watcher had seen Spring Foot visit the boy. The evidence against him was overwhelming and because he had pleaded innocent, the elders showed him no mercy. Afterwards, Mamm gathered up what was left of her brother and buried his remains under the broken oak tree. The ground took him deep and fast and held him there. For all her weeping and pleading, he never came back.

Mamm's heart constricts. She would give anything to run with him through the soft dappled light of the forest or lie with him under the stars, dreaming about the places they'd go if they were free. She's grieved so many brothers and sisters over the years (Pine Thwack, Leaf Wart, Green Beard, Twice Dew), and each one pained her greatly, but none hurt so badly as losing Spring Foot.

Eventually she stops and straightens her aching back. Before her is a flight of stone steps leading up to an imposing double door. The courthouse is the only structure standing in the rubble, though its once pristine white walls are now rough and dirty. There was a time when witnessing the demise of her masters would have lifted her spirits, but she's too wearied by grief to rejoice in destruction.

A shimmer of movement makes her pause. Scuttling over the walls are hundreds of black spiders, each one with a single large eyeball for a body. More of her masters' creations sent to spy on her. She steps forward and they pour down the walls, all of them whispering.

'Bow your head before your masters, spriggan.'

'An end to her!'

'Useless spriggan, just like the rest of them.'

'Send her to ground!'

Mamm's knee pains her. She quickly readjusts the pine cone there and stands tall. She has to stay strong. Drawing back her shoulders, she knocks on the door: three good hard raps that say she has nothing to hide and isn't afraid.

The door opens and Mamm glances around the

empty courtroom, quaking inside. It looks exactly how it did all those years ago. Most of the space is taken up with red-and-white-spotted toadstools arranged in concentric circles. Garlands of ivy and gold festoon the wood-panelled walls and the place blazes with candlelight. From the ceiling hang three chandeliers, fashioned from the spines of deer and dripping with red cut glass, the crystals glinting like bloodied knives. Animal skulls adorn the walls, a candle placed within each open jaw. Every now and then hot wax patters to the floor, filling the air with a rich smoky haze.

At the back of the room is a raised wooden platform, and on it a row of desks, ready for the elders to take their places. A door creaks open to her left and a giant black spider, about half her height, scuttles in. Mamm eyes it nervously as it positions itself behind a desk piled high with papers. Like the spiders outside, its body is made up of a single bulging eyeball, blinking and bloodshot.

The arachnid beckons her forward with one hairy black leg. She walks into the centre and pauses where Spring Foot once stood. The spider sighs with something like impatience, then picks up the papers and shuffles them from limb to limb. Eventually it stops and announces, 'Court in session!'

The seven elders appear behind their desks, popping into existence one by one, sitting atop their toadstools. While the rest of their kind have long silver hair and dress in rags, the elders' hair is black and they wear tweed suits with ceremonial chains about their necks, strings of teeth not eased from beneath the pillows of sleeping children, but taken from their victims as trophies.

The elders check the papers before them with bowed heads. Occasionally they stretch their leathery wings and lean towards one another, muttering. A couple glance up and Mamm flinches. Their glowing white eyes bore into her and she thinks of a finger prodding a tender spot, searching for a weakness.

Turning to the courtroom, the spider blinks before commanding, 'Rise for the elders!'

The rest of her masters make themselves visible, and Mamm is surprised to see so few of them. Three quarters of the toadstool seats are empty. She knows their numbers have dwindled over the years, but surely this can't be all that's left?

The spider points an accusing limb in her direction. 'Mamm Spriggan, you know the rules of court; plead guilty to your crime and the elders may give you a chance to redeem yourself, but if you protest your innocence and are found guilty, death will be final. Do you understand?'

Mamm nods, barely able to speak.

'I need an answer.'

Her voice is small and strained. 'Yes, I understand.'

The spider's eye glances around the room then blinks and swivels in her direction. 'Mamm Spriggan, you stand before the court of elders accused of dereliction of duty. A girl who trespassed on the glade has returned – because you failed to frighten her away. How do you plead?'

Mamm's shoulders drop. There's only one answer she can give.

14

Pippa clutched the covers, caught in that delicate and dangerous place between sleep and waking. Something sinister was prowling the edges of her mind, watching her with glowing white eyes. A charred twig hand emerged from a pile of leaves and the ground gave way beneath her. The hidden folk crawled towards her on all sides, their eyes shining in the gloom. 'No,' she murmured. 'Leave me alone.' She turned over and a harsh voice whispered in her ear. 'Trespass against us and we'll trespass against you.'

She opened her eyes, her pulse racing. Something had startled her from sleep; a noise – but what? She lay still, listening to the moan of the wind outside and the occasional tap of vines against the window pane. At least, that's what she thought it was. A faint smell of smoke filled her nose and she found herself thinking of the twig men.

Tap. Tap. Tap. So quiet she wondered if she'd imagined it.

Someone's in the room with you.

The thought wormed its way into her mind and refused to leave. Holding her breath, she lowered the covers and peered into the blackness. She couldn't see anything, yet she knew for certain that she wasn't alone. The dark bristled with energy, but it didn't feel exciting and full of possibility. It felt as if someone – or *something* – was staring back at her. The tapping started again, and her muscles tensed. The sound was coming from above her.

She sat up and something sharp scratched her cheek. Picturing clawed black fingers, she yelped and shot out of bed. She was almost at the door when pain stabbed at the bare soles of her feet. She switched on the light and her cries died in her throat.

The room was full of twig men. There were even more of them than before, crowding the window and hanging over her bed. Only this time they were black as if they'd been burnt by fire. Several were dangling upside down by their ankles, their arms reaching towards her pillow. How long had they been there? The thought of them touching her while she slept made her feel sick.

She stepped back and a fresh stab of pain bit into her foot. Several of her glass jars lay smashed on the floor, the jagged shards strewn across the carpet.

Laughter sounded behind her and a husky voice whispered in her ear. 'We warned you – stay away from Whispering Hollow!' A pile of books toppled from her desk and something scurried under her bed.

'Jed!' She hobbled out to the landing and shouted again. 'Help! Jed!'

He opened his door and blinked at her sleepily.

'There's something in my … It …' she gasped, unable to get the words out.

'What's the matter? What's happened?' He saw her bloodied feet and his face paled. 'Grandpa!' he yelled. 'Come quick, Newt's hurt!' He started to go downstairs, but Pippa clutched his top. She didn't want to be left alone, not even for a moment.

Grandpa appeared at the bottom of the gloomy stairway and switched on the light. He called up to them, his voice shaking. 'What is it? What's there?'

'It's my foot,' cried Pippa. 'My jars are broken.'

Grandpa grabbed the banister and hauled himself up, wincing with each step. 'Don't move! If there's glass in your foot it will make it worse.'

Pippa sat on the landing while Grandpa awkwardly lowered himself to one knee. 'This may hurt a bit,' he warned. Before she had time to think, he pulled a piece of glass from her foot. A rush of blood seeped out and a hot queasy feeling washed over her. He rubbed his beard and sucked in a breath. 'Jed, there's a first-aid kit under the sink.'

'I'll get it,' he said, already charging down the stairs.

A few seconds later he returned and held out the small green bag, his left cheek twitching with anxiety. Grandpa took out an antiseptic wipe and cleaned her foot, then applied a plaster and a bandage. 'It's not deep enough to need stitches. You'll be all right.'

Pippa nodded, feeling a little better. It was only then that she noticed her grandfather was fully dressed. He must have been sleeping downstairs on the sofa. He pushed himself up to standing and rubbed his knee with a grimace. 'How did your jars get broken?'

Pippa looked away. She knew she had to tell him everything, even though it would mean getting into trouble for entering the glade. First, though, she wanted Jed to see her room. He hadn't believed her about the hidden folk and he probably wouldn't believe her if she told him about the voice she'd heard either. But when he saw the twig men, he'd know that Grandpa couldn't have left them there. His knee was so bad, there's no way he could have made it up and down the stairs several times in the night, never mind clamber on to a chair and attach them to the ceiling.

'I could really do with a hot chocolate. Can we talk downstairs?' asked Pippa.

'OK.' He smiled at her kindly. 'You get dressed and I'll make you both a drink.'

Pippa got to her feet and Grandpa put his arms around her and Jed. He kissed the tops of their heads and held them tightly, as if he never wanted to let them go. Eventually he turned away and made his way downstairs.

Pippa crossed the landing, relieved to find her foot didn't hurt too much, and pointed at her door. 'Look!' she said.

Jed went into her room. She expected him to shout in surprise, but instead he sounded confused. 'What am I supposed to be looking at?'

'The twig men!'

Pippa followed after him and blinked in disbelief. They were gone.

'But they were here! I woke up and the room was full of them!'

Jed sighed impatiently. 'Things don't magically appear and disappear, Newt. You must have been dreaming.' Careful to avoid the broken glass on her floor, he walked over to the window, which was now inexplicably wide open. Pulling it closed, he added more gently, 'When you're half asleep, it's easy to imagine things.'

She lifted a finger to her cheek and felt a scratch mark. It was real. Whatever had been in her room – and whatever that *thing* outside was – it must be able to turn invisible. That would explain why she hadn't been able to see anything just now and in the glade without her binoculars. Somehow, they allowed her to see it. If only they'd recorded it too.

Jed gave her a wary look and headed for the door. 'See you in the kitchen.'

Pippa grabbed her clothes from the back of the chair and hurriedly got dressed. Even if Jed didn't believe her about the hidden folk, she had a feeling Grandpa would.

15

The children entered the kitchen and were surprised to see the back door had been boarded up with planks of wood. Grandpa went to the window and checked outside. The dawn sky was swollen with rainclouds, a livid bruise of purple and black slashed through with pink.

Pippa touched his arm. She didn't want to tell him about the hidden folk, because then she'd have to admit she'd been in the glade. But she had to find out if he knew about them too. 'What's going on, Grandpa? Why are you so afraid? Is there something out there?'

He pulled out a chair and sat down heavily, as if all the energy had been drained from him.

'Grandpa, you have to tell us,' insisted Pippa.

His face crumpled. 'What I'm about to say will be hard to believe.'

The children took a seat opposite him and Pippa

leaned forward. She was so apprehensive she felt as if a hummingbird was beating its wings inside her chest.

'I didn't tell you before because I didn't want to frighten you. But things are getting worse and you need to know the truth for your own safety.' Grandpa laid his palms flat on the table. 'You know I grew up in this house, don't you?' The children nodded and he continued, 'Well, when I was young – about the same age as you are now, Pippa – I had a strange experience, one that has stayed with me all my life.'

He glanced at the ceiling. 'I was in my bed one night when something climbed through my window. He was like a man with a head and arms and legs, but he was made of branches and had a big mossy beard and bushy green feet.'

Jed slumped back in his chair, a look of disappointment and anger on his face.

Grandpa spoke quickly, as if desperate to win their trust. 'I was afraid, terrified even. I wanted to shout for my parents, but then he spoke to me and ...' He rubbed his chin and let out a heavy breath. 'I can't explain it, but there was kindness in his voice. Even though I was scared, I was mesmerised by him. He told me he'd seen me go into the glade and touch the stone earlier that day. He warned me to stay away from it. I must never touch it or climb on it, or crawl into the hole beneath it, or something terrible would happen.'

Pippa's eyes widened. Questions buzzed in her head, but she didn't dare interrupt. She desperately wanted to hear the rest of the story.

'He visited me every night that week. I grew less afraid and we chatted for hours. I don't remember what about exactly, only that it was silly things: whether worms dream when they sleep, what frost smells like, how the moon got its face. I was a lonely lad growing up, always sneaking off to the forest when I should have been at school, and I enjoyed his company. I remember he laughed often and loud, a wonderful deep rumble that made you want to laugh with him. One evening Ma woke up and came into my room and the man – or whatever he was – disappeared. I stayed awake for hours that night, but he never came back.'

Grandpa pinched the bridge of his nose. 'After that, bad things began to happen in the house. The sugar was switched for salt, the milk would turn sour overnight, and things would go missing. Of course, I got the blame for everything.'

Pippa nodded, realising why he'd been relieved when the sugar tasted normal and the milk hadn't gone off yesterday.

'Once, I woke up to find a small twig man on my pillow,' he continued. 'I kept it for a while, but I don't know what happened to it over the years. The trouble stopped as quickly as it started a few weeks later and life went on as before, but I always wondered about the man. When my parents died, they left the place to me, but by then I'd moved to London and was settled there. Then, after your grandma passed away, I felt an urge to come back. I missed the woods and I suppose I wanted to see if the man would visit me again.'

'And did he?' asked Pippa.

'No, but I still think about him, even though I try to put it out of my mind.'

'You're out of your mind, all right,' muttered Jed.

Pippa elbowed her brother then turned back to their grandfather and raised her voice. 'You know when we came last time and I saw a strange woman on my window ledge, had you seen her too? Is that why you took us back to London?'

'What woman?' Jed asked, sounding shocked.

'No, I only ever saw a man.' Grandpa looked down and swallowed. 'I hated seeing you so frightened that night. I never imagined anything would appear to one of you, not after all these years. Just because the man was friendly to me, doesn't mean others of his kind would be the same. I was afraid the woman might appear again and hurt you. I couldn't take the risk, so I drove you home.'

Pippa took a moment to let the information sink in. 'Do you think the woman left the twig men in the house?'

'No, at least I don't think so. The way the man talked, it was like he was trying to protect me. I think he was warning me to stay away from the stone because something else would hurt me.'

'Like what?' demanded Jed.

Grandpa turned to the window and his eyes glazed over, his mind seemingly elsewhere. 'I wish it weren't true, but there are horrible things in this world, wicked things.'

Pippa's arms prickled with goose bumps. She glanced at Jed and then back to their grandfather. 'What kind of things, Grandpa?'

'I believe there are hidden folk living in Whispering Hollow. I haven't seen them, but I've heard them moving around the house at night. I think they're the ones who bring in the twig men.'

Jed snorted with exasperation. 'Hidden folk again!'

Grandpa fixed him with a stern look. 'Hidden folk, fae, faeries, call them what you will, but there have been stories about such things living in these parts for centuries. Whatever they are, I can tell you this

117

much – they are cruel. It's because of them I fell over and damaged my knee.'

'How?' asked Jed, his voice briefly cracking and going high. 'You said you hadn't seen them!'

'A few days after I took you back to London, I had a nap and when I woke up the room was dark. So dark, I didn't notice my shoelaces had been tied together. I think they broke Pippa's jars so that she would step on the glass. I'm telling you this so you know to be careful.'

'I believe you,' said Pippa. 'Last night I—'

Jed shoved back his chair and stood up. 'Suppose they exist, which they *don't*. Why would they fill the house with twig figures?'

Grandpa rubbed his head. 'I don't have all the answers, but I used the library computer to read about them once. I know hidden folk don't like to be seen, and going near their land or taking their treasure angers them. In the past, people would knock the corners from their houses if they thought it blocked a faerie path. Even their trees were considered dangerous to chop down. One thorn tree in Scotland was left standing, even though it prevented a road from being widened for seventy years.'

He paused then added, 'Why the twig men, I don't know. It started after I took you back home that night.

I tried taking the figures outside. I piled them up in the woods, but they only brought more of them into the house, and then the leaves and moss and mushrooms started to appear. I was worried burning them might make things worse, but I didn't know what else to do. Afterwards I had a bad feeling about it, that's why I let you visit Ollie. I thought you'd be safer if you were away from the house.'

'Is that why you've been wearing your clothes inside out?' asked Pippa.

'Sorry, I didn't catch that?'

She spoke up and he looked at her in surprise. 'Yes. It's meant to keep them away, but I'm not sure it works.'

Pippa nodded, relieved things were starting to make sense. The voice had said, *Trespass against us and we'll trespass against you.* Maybe they were angry because she'd touched the stone in summer. If they didn't want to be seen, leaving the twig men would be their way of trespassing where she lived.

Jed turned and headed to the door. 'I've had enough of this.'

'Where are you going?' called Grandpa.

'For a walk!'

Grandpa started to go after him, then stopped and clutched his leg. He turned to Pippa, his voice choked.

'You have to stop him. Don't let him go into the glade.'

The front door slammed and Pippa jumped to her feet. She wanted to tell her grandfather what she'd seen and how she thought the hidden folk had been in her room, but it would have to wait.

16

Pippa ran out of the house and searched the shadowy garden. Jed was standing by the broken oak tree, kicking its trunk. He saw her coming and headed for the bushes that marked the entrance to the glade. 'Wait! It's not safe!' she called.

He stopped and spun round. 'Just because Grandpa made up some stupid story doesn't mean it's true.'

'But Grandpa didn't make it up,' she said, hurrying towards him and speaking through snatched breaths. 'I've seen things too.'

'*Faeries?*' He laughed. 'Come on, Newt.'

Pippa balled her hands into fists.

A crow flew overhead with a loud *caw* then landed on a nearby bush, seeming to watch them. Pippa shivered. Neither of them had stopped to put on a coat and it was freezing. 'Please, Jed, let's go back. We can talk about it inside.'

'Talk about what?' he scoffed. 'How there are little

creatures with wings living in the glade? Or how tree men with big mossy beards are breaking and entering through people's windows?'

Pippa's cheeks burned despite the cold. She knew it was hard to believe – she might not have believed it herself if she hadn't seen it with her own eyes – but why did he have to be so stubborn? 'We can talk about whatever you want,' she said, trying her best to sound calm. 'But let's go inside.'

'You're scared, aren't you? You think that if I touch the stone something bad will happen. Well, it won't and I'll prove it to you!'

'Don't, Jed! I'm cold. Please, I want to go back.'

Ignoring her pleas, he turned and shoved his way through the dense bushes. Pippa stamped her foot in frustration. Her instincts told her to run back to the house, but what if there were more hidden folk in the glade? She couldn't leave him.

Cursing, she pushed her way through the leafy branches then blinked in surprise. Jed was standing in front of the stone. He looked strange in the half-light, too tall and too thin, and for a split second she almost didn't recognise him. Cold foggy air swirled about them, briefly obscuring their faces. It wasn't just the churning mist that filled Pippa with foreboding. The opening beneath the stone didn't look right, the

122

blackness seeming to pulsate and grow darker. She blinked and the hole appeared normal, yet she couldn't shake the feeling it had grown bigger.

Jed pressed his palms to the stone and a rumble of thunder sounded in the distance. 'Hey, hidden folk!' he shouted. 'Come and show yourselves!' Pippa turned and stared in every direction, wishing she had her binoculars. There could be dozens of creatures surrounding them right now and they wouldn't know. They had to get out of here.

'I'm going!' she announced, hoping Jed might follow her back to the house. She started to leave, when he crouched down. Reaching inside the hole, he groped around then pulled out his hand. 'Look,' he said. 'Faerie treasure!'

'Put it back,' warned Pippa, moving towards him.

'Maybe it's a ruby,' he teased, holding up the chunk of red glass. 'Hey! I've stolen your treasure!' he shouted to the air. 'Aren't you going to come and get it?'

The wind shook the trees above, filling the air with a sinister whispering sound. Tears stung Pippa's eyes. She jumped up and snatched the glass from him. 'Stop being an idiot! You don't understand what you're doing!' she cried, throwing the glass back into the hole.

Jed's cheek twitched. '*I'm* an idiot? You're the one who's crying like a five-year-old because I don't believe in faeries.'

Pippa shoved him. 'I'm trying to help you!'

'Help me? You'd *help me* if you didn't keep asking me to play with you. You'd help me if you stopped going on about your stupid binoculars. You'd help me if you didn't embarrass me in front of my friends!'

Pippa stepped back, feeling shaky and unsure of herself. Is that how he saw her: an annoying little brat who followed him around? Ollie was her friend too and she hadn't meant to embarrass him. She'd said gaming was boring because they'd laughed at her for reading about faeries. And the only reason she'd suggested checking on the den was because she thought Jed would enjoy it. More than anything, she wanted the brother she knew back: the one who played with her, and made her laugh, and explained things when she didn't understand. 'Why do you have to be so mean?' she asked through tears. 'You never used to be like this.'

Jed sighed. 'People change. *Some* of us grow up.'

'That's not fair.'

'Life *isn't* fair.' He glared at her, his eyes dark with resentment. 'It's OK for you. All *you've* got to worry about is faeries.'

Pippa recoiled. It felt like he was trying to find new ways to confuse and hurt her. Why? What had she ever done to him? She wiped her eyes then lurched away and stumbled in the long grass. Holding the stone to steady herself, she let out a sob. 'I wish I had a different brother,' she said, meaning it with all her heart.

Thunder boomed overhead.

She ran out of the glade and didn't look back to see Jed's face. She didn't care if she'd hurt him. Right then, she didn't care about him at all.

17

Mamm lowers her gaze. She's ashamed to bow her head before the elders, but what choice does she have? If she protests her innocence, they'll call the crow watcher as witness. He'll recount how she failed to stop the humans burning the twig men and it will only sour the elders' mood against her.

'I plead guilty,' she whispers.

An excited hush falls over the room as the elders lean close and debate her fate. She can guess what they're saying: they created her for a purpose and that is to defend their realm. If Mamm had scared the girl away, the child would never have returned to the forest. And now she and her family dared to burn their warnings!

The elders pucker their faces and shake their heads. Mamm shifts under their piercing white gaze. If they knew the truth, they would end her right now. Her power to frighten children has been waning for years, so few humans are able to see her these days.

She thinks about the first time she laid eyes on the girl. She'd been overcome with rage and had wanted to terrify the child, just as she was created to do. But when she saw her playing outside, so wild and free, she was taken with the notion that she might be different. She allowed herself to hope the child might see her, that she might speak to her. And she *had* seen her.

Mamm's eyes sting and she presses her palms to her face. *Silly old fool, what were you thinking? Your kind will never be free.*

One of the elders picks up a feathered quill and writes on a piece of scroll paper, before passing it down the line of desks. The spider scuttles over and its eyeball roves from left to right as it reads. The audience murmurs and fidgets on their toadstools. Aside from the occasional splutter of hot candle wax, the room is silent.

The arachnid clears its throat. 'Mamm Spriggan, you have been offered the chance to redeem yourself . . .'

'No!' shouts one of the masters in the audience.

'She failed us!' cries another.

'To the ground with her!'

The spider turns to face the room. 'Silence in court!' The crowd grumbles and eventually grows quiet. The arachnid continues. '*If* you complete the task successfully then you shall be pardoned. Fail and death will be final.'

More shouts go up for her to die and Mamm steadies herself. She's heard enough stories over the years to know the task will be near impossible. Suddenly she wants done with the whole charade. Why should she grasp at hope and humiliate herself for her masters' pleasure?

She nods and drops her gaze.

'You must complete the task in full,' the spider says. 'Fail, and death will be—'

Mamm bristles as he completes the sentence. *Final. Yes, I got that part.*

'Mamm Spriggan. Your task is to . . .'

Just then the walls of the courtroom begin to tremble. A deep rumbling sounds as plaster showers down from the ceiling. Shouts of alarm fill the room and several elders jump to their feet. They move their arms, drawing lines and dots with their magic, and the walls stop shaking.

Calm has barely been restored when the courtroom doors burst open. The crow watcher flaps its wings and caws loudly. Mamm isn't pleased to see the bird, even if it's a relief to see a normal-sized creature with eyeballs where they should be.

'A boy is in the glade!' cries the crow. 'He's out there now *caw* with the girl.'

The elders retake their seats except for one who remains standing. Badnerjak. He is much taller than the others and wears twice as many chains of teeth. Mamm remembers the last time she saw him. The elders may have condemned Spring Foot by committee, but Badnerjak was the one who took his life.

'What have they done to cause this disturbance?' he demands, speaking directly to the crow, all pomp and ceremony forgotten.

The crow caws and hops excitedly. 'The girl made a wish upon the stone.'

Badnerjak sneers at Mamm as if this new turn of events is somehow her fault. Licking his lips, he leans forward and peers at the bird. 'Tell me, what did the girl wish for exactly?'

Mamm nibbles on a thread of sackcloth inside her cheek. She has no idea what the girl said, but from the way the crow caws at her accusingly she has a bad feeling about it.

'Well?' asks Badnerjak. The bird turns its head this way and that, its dark eyes flashing, but stays put. Badnerjak thumps the desk and the crow caws with alarm and flies over. 'I asked you a question, watcher. You would do well to answer me.'

The reply comes in a croaked whisper. 'She asked for a *caw* different brother.'

'And then what happened?'

The crow tilts its head as if unsure. 'The girl returned to the house.'

'And the boy?'

'I . . . I don't know.'

'Speak up for the benefit of the court!'

The crow repeats itself and Badnerjak makes a show of surveying the audience before turning back to the bird. 'You don't know because you didn't watch to see where he went.'

'I *caw* . . . I wanted to bring you word straight away.'

Badnerjak shouts, making the bird jump. 'You *dared* to come here and interrupt official court proceedings with half a story!'

'It's the spriggan's fault! *Caw* if she'd frightened the girl when—'

Badnerjak raises a long, pale finger to his lips, silencing the bird, and Mamm sags with relief. The court is well aware of her crime; she doesn't need the crow reminding them.

'This is not the first time you've failed us, is it, watcher?'

Before the crow can answer, Badnerjak grabs it around the neck. A furious flapping of wings ensues, feathers flying everywhere. He grapples with the panicked bird for several long seconds before closing both hands about its wings and raising it into the air.

Fear blazes in the crow's eyes.

Badnerjak squeezes tighter.

Crick-crack. The bird's tiny bones snap.

Mamm's heart thumps against her ribcage. It feels as if fingers are pressing into her throat and she can't breathe. A memory flashes into her mind and she shuts her eyes . . .

Spring Foot stands in the centre of the courtroom: a huge, towering figure, his body covered with lush green branches, his feet sprouting bushy spruce pine. The audience is packed with masters, all of them shouting and jeering. The spider steps forward. 'The elders have reached a verdict!' it announces.

A cheer goes up and Spring Foot stands tall and pulls back his shoulders. He spots Mamm in the crowd and nods at her. Anyone who didn't know him would think he was fearless, but Mamm sees the flicker of anxiety in his eyes, the sudden waver of his smile. She holds her breath, the wait unbearable. Seconds which feel like hours pass . . .

'Guilty!' exclaims the spider.

Spring Foot looks to Mamm, the shock on his face turning to terror. His eyes plead silently, but she is powerless. Mamm's knees buckle and her sisters catch her arms on either side. She wants to scream, but her voice is trapped in her throat. She wants to take him away from this hateful place, but her legs won't move.

Badnerjak strides forward and raises his right arm. As he does, Spring Foot drops to his knees with a crack. A mighty tree felled in one strike. Badnerjak grabs him about the throat and sucks out his life. It happens so fast. One moment he is there: her magnificent, glorious brother. And then he falls apart and all that remains of him is a pile of branches.

Mamm takes a trembling breath and opens her eyes, back in the present once more. She's relived the moment her brother was killed a thousand times over. Why didn't she *do* something? She should have begged the elders to take her life and spare his.

Feeling helpless, she watches as the bird's eyes grow dull. Like a delinquent child unsatisfied by the suffering of its victim, Badnerjak shakes the crow and smiles when it begins to struggle once more.

Mamm turns her head away and what she sees sickens her. The masters lean forwards in their seats, grinning and licking their lips, their chests heaving with excitement.

CRACK.

Badnerjak breaks the bird's neck and its beak opens, releasing a stream of white mist into the air. He drinks it down greedily. Once done, he plucks a single black feather from the bird then tosses its lifeless body to the floor. As soon as the crow hits the ground, its body splinters into a cloud of dust. What once appeared to be a bird is revealed in its true form: a heap of twigs, damp earth and moss.

Mamm wraps her arms around herself, feeling as if she's been dealt a blow. She's seen the elders extract the quickening from their creations before, and it always shakes her to her core. Watchers are not sent to ground, only spriggan. But it is nothing like this. Spriggans fall apart in their sleep, their bodies slowly disintegrating into the earth before being called back to life. But when the elders terminate a life the result is swift and brutal.

Death is *final*.

Badnerjak wipes his mouth then takes a seat and passes the feather to his companions. Each one falls on it hungrily, sniffing and snorting as if trying to inhale every last trace of the bird's essence. Mamm has never witnessed her masters create life, but she knows a piece of the original is always needed to form a new being. Perhaps the next watcher won't fail them.

The spider scuttles over to the line of desks, its bulging eyeball noticeably more bloodshot than before. 'And the spriggan . . . ?' it asks warily, placing the scroll on the desk.

Badnerjak snatches the scroll and rips it in two.

A new task is written down and passed along the row of desks to the spider. The elders pat each other on the back then turn to Mamm and grin. Whatever they have planned, she knows it will be meant to hurt her.

18

Pippa ran back to the house then trudged into the kitchen and hung her head. 'I tried,' she said, throwing herself into a chair. Grandpa stood up and anxiously looked behind her.

'Where's your brother?'

'In the glade.'

'Say again?'

'He's in the glade! I tried to stop him but he wouldn't listen.'

Grandpa gripped the edge of the table, his body swaying unsteadily. Seeing the look of fear in his eyes made Pippa feel even more helpless. 'I'm sorry,' she said.

'It's not your fault. I'll go and find him.'

Pippa's tummy clenched with guilt. Grandpa didn't know about the creature she'd seen. If she'd told him how it had killed a poor mouse, he'd be frantic with worry.

'Grandpa . . .' she started. Her throat was tight and

it was hard to get the words out. 'There's something I need to tell you.'

'What did you say? Speak up, I can't hear.'

She dropped her head, afraid to see the look of hurt and disappointment on his face when she told him she'd touched the stone in the summer and gone to Whispering Hollow again last night. 'I've done something . . .' she eventually managed. Before she could finish the sentence, Grandpa lifted her chin. She felt so awful she was sure he must be able to see the guilt written on her face, but when she raised her gaze she saw only love and concern.

'I have some news,' he said. 'I left a message on your dad's phone after you hurt your foot, saying you'd had an accident and it was an emergency. He called back while you were out looking for Jed. Your mum has to stay to oversee the movers, but he'll be here this afternoon.'

'Really?' asked Pippa. 'But I thought the landline wasn't working?'

Grandpa reached for his coat and coughed. 'I might have accidentally unplugged it after your father left a message to say he was bringing you both here. He wanted to talk to you just now, but I made out you couldn't get to the phone. I'm afraid I exaggerated about your foot a bit, so don't be surprised if he expects you to have broken a few toes when he gets here.'

'What about you, Grandpa? Will you come back with us?'

'Don't worry about me.' He huffed. 'I'll get by.'

'But you can't stay here!' She was about to insist that he came to London with them when the front door opened and then banged closed.

'Jed, is that you?' called Grandpa.

They listened to him stomp up the stairs and then slam his bedroom door.

'At least we know where he is,' said Grandpa.

Pippa's heart filled with relief. Part of her wanted to run up to Jed's room and tell him the good news that Dad was on his way, but what if he was mean to her again?

Grandpa smiled. 'I'll make us some breakfast.'

'It's OK, I'll do it,' said Pippa.

He shuffled over and patted her shoulder. 'Thank you, but I need to keep moving or I'll seize up completely.'

While Grandpa made tea, Pippa looked in the fridge. Apart from a small chunk of cheese and a few squashed tomatoes, it was empty.

'I'm afraid there isn't enough milk for cereal,' said Grandpa.

Pippa opened the door to the pantry. There was a large bag of pasta shells, a few tins of vegetables, and only four slices of bread left.

Grandpa stirred two mugs of tea. 'I'm a bit low on food, sorry; getting to the shops isn't easy with my knee and I didn't want to get the bus into town and leave you kids here alone.'

'That's OK, Grandpa. Toast is my favourite anyway,' Pippa said, popping two slices of bread into the toaster as she watched her grandfather pick up the mugs and limp back to the table. Seeing him struggle made her heart ache. Grandpa had been living with the hidden folk coming into the house for months and had fallen and hurt his knee because of them. If she'd done as she was told and not gone into the glade, none of this would have happened.

Even if she couldn't face telling him the truth, she could make sure he came back to London with them. Grandpa was so stubborn though. After his fall, Dad had asked him to move in with them so they could take care of him, and he'd refused. It had ended in an argument, as it always did with them. If Grandpa refused to leave, she'd need to persuade Dad that he couldn't be allowed to stay in the house. But Jed hadn't believed her about the hidden folk and she was sure Dad wouldn't either. There was only one way to convince them they were real – she needed proof.

Pippa couldn't shake the feeling the binoculars might have recorded the creature on a different setting. Perhaps if she went into town Ollie's cousin could help.

'I'll go to the supermarket for you,' said Pippa. 'I don't mind.'

'Thank you, but I think you should wait here for your father to arrive.'

Before Pippa had a chance to try and persuade him, Jed came into the room. He walked over to the toaster and shoved both slices of toast into his mouth. Then he opened the fridge and ate the last of the cheese and the tomatoes.

Grandpa smiled. 'Your brother's going through another growth spurt, I see.'

Pippa shrugged, feeding the last two slices of bread into the toaster for her and Grandpa. As far as she could tell, Jed was just being selfish. She watched him search through the cupboards then take out a tin of peas. He shook the can and she had a feeling he might eat them next. Seeing him so hungry gave her an idea.

'It will be hours until Dad arrives and we're both starving. *Please*, Grandpa.'

'Let me think about it,' he grumbled.

The wind picked up outside, rattling the windows in their frames. Grandpa startled and she realised why he'd been so jumpy yesterday. It must be exhausting living in fear of things coming into your house. Pippa didn't like being sneaky, but going into town was her only chance to prove the hidden folk were real. She *had* to persuade Dad to make Grandpa come back with them. She raised her voice and tried to sound scared. 'What you told us before . . . I'm not sure I like being in the house.'

He stared at the back door as if fearful it might blow open. 'Hmm. It might be safer for you in town than here,' he muttered.

Pippa went over and kissed him. 'Thanks, Grandpa. I won't be long.'

'Wait, I didn't say . . .' He saw the disappointed look on her face and grunted. 'All right, I suppose you can go. Jed, you'll get the bus into town with your sister and get my groceries, won't you?'

Pippa bit her fingernail. She didn't want to go anywhere with her brother and he'd made it perfectly clear he didn't want to spend any time with *her*.

'Sure, I'll go,' said Jed. 'It'll be fun.'

Pippa expected him to roll his eyes or say something sarcastic under his breath, but he didn't. There wasn't a trace of meanness on his face.

'Good boy,' said Grandpa. 'You'd best get a move on; the bus goes in fifteen minutes. You're not to go anywhere else, no venturing into the forest or visiting your friend up the lane. I want you back before your father arrives.'

'Dad's coming?' asked Jed.

'He'll be here by teatime if he has a good run,' said Grandpa. He stood and took his wallet from his pocket, then counted out some notes. 'That should be enough to cover it – and ten pounds each for going. I've already started a list; I just need to add a few things to it.'

Pippa ran upstairs and stashed her binoculars in her rucksack, then came back down and put on her coat and baseball cap. Grandpa gave the money and shopping list to her brother, and then limped after them into the hallway. Touching Jed's shoulder, he lowered his voice. 'What I told you before . . . I know it's a lot to take in. I'm just asking you to keep an open mind. Can you do that for me?'

Jed blinked at him as if his earlier outburst had never happened. 'Of course,' he said with a smile. Grandpa patted him on the back and Pippa looked from one to the other, unsure what was happening. Whatever weird game Jed was playing she didn't buy it for one second. As soon as they were on the bus, she fully expected him to go back to being horrible.

19

Mamm slumps against the cave wall, her limbs shaking with fatigue. She knew the first part of the task would be difficult, but she hadn't realised how much of her strength it would take.

Stupid spriggan, you did this to yourself.

She hits her palm against her forehead, angry at herself for not dealing with the girl the moment she touched the stone. Instead she allowed herself to be swept up in a fantasy, hoping the child might offer up her name.

Mamm doesn't want to hurt the children any more than she already has, but she must if she wants to survive. Nothing can save the girl now, or her brother.

19

20

The children arrived at the bus stop just in time. They had barely had a chance to catch their breath when the bright-green bus to Penwith rumbled down the lane. As soon as they'd bought their tickets, the vehicle lurched forward so that they had to grab on to the nearest seat to stop from falling over. The only other passengers, a grey-haired couple who were arguing over a map, didn't look up as they went to the back and sat down.

Pippa turned her body away and stared outside. Jed didn't say a word. She presumed he was playing something, but then she noticed he wasn't holding anything in his hands. His coat, which was draped over his lap, didn't appear to have anything in the pockets either. He'd only gone back for the jacket because Grandpa had reminded him, but it wasn't like him to leave his Switch behind. He always took it with him.

'I'm going to spend my money in the fudge shop,' said Jed.

Pippa eyed him warily.

'Or that sweet shop on the corner, you know, with all the jars in the window.'

She remembered the giant stripy bags of pick 'n' mix they'd bought in the summer. They'd tasted so good it was worth getting an extra filling at the dentist.

Jed licked his lips. 'I'm going to buy a bag of gobstoppers and some sherbet lemons and strawberry bonbons, and . . . what were those little yellow ones called again?'

'Pear drops,' said Pippa, momentarily forgetting that she wasn't speaking to him unless it was absolutely necessary.

'Yes!' said Jed. 'Do you remember the time we stashed a bag of sweets in the tree house so Grandpa wouldn't see?'

Pippa tensed. Was this some kind of trick? To remind her of the fun they'd had and then say something mean? But the only sound Jed made came from his tummy. It grumbled so loudly that the couple in front stopped bickering and briefly turned round.

'They could use a gobstopper or two,' whispered Jed a little too loudly.

Pippa giggled and covered her mouth. She felt uncomfortable laughing, not just because two grown-ups were glaring at them, but because she and Jed hadn't made up after their fight. Was he going to apologise or say anything, she wondered, or simply act like it had never happened? As the bus made its way along the narrow winding lanes, he chatted about their previous trips to the beach and his favourite shops in town. Pippa didn't add much to the conversation – she still hadn't forgiven him for the hurtful things he'd said – but listening to him was better than sitting in angry silence. It had been ages since Jed had talked to her so freely, and for now at least it felt like a peace offering.

When the bus arrived at Penwith twenty minutes later it was raining steadily. The children waited for the couple to get off then went to the front and thanked the driver. Stepping on to the pavement, Pippa was assaulted by a gust of cold sea air. Ominous black clouds dominated the sky, casting the world in shadow. Even the buildings painted an assortment of pastel colours – turquoise, pink and lemon – struggled to provide some cheer to the day.

Maybe it was talking about other times they'd visited, but Pippa was shocked to see the town looking so empty. The narrow high street had been heaving with tourists in summer, but now it was practically deserted. The only other people were two women sharing an umbrella and clutching each other by the arm as if afraid they might be swept off their feet. Pippa noticed that Jed still wasn't wearing his coat. 'Aren't you cold?' she asked. He stopped to put on his jacket then hurried to catch up with her.

Ollie had said he was going to be helping Taylor in the bookstore today. There was only one bookshop in town and it was on the promenade, just before the supermarket. As she marched down the hill, Pippa decided that she and Jed needed to split up – she would go to the bookstore while he bought the groceries. She didn't want him around while she talked to Ollie's cousin. Pippa had rehearsed what she was going to say: she'd recorded a fox at night and needed some help to retrieve the footage. The last thing she wanted was Jed talking about the hidden folk and trying to embarrass her.

They turned left on to the promenade and the wind pounced on them like an animal, tugging at their hair and clothes and pushing them back. The fudge shop had a *closed* sign in the window and the emporium selling seaside trinkets and beach toys was in total darkness; no bright-yellow blow-up dinghies, racks of wetsuits, or tubs of colourful buckets and spades outside. The only things on the pavement were two seagulls having a staring contest over a squashed chip.

More noisy gulls circled high above, their bodies blown and buffeted by the icy gusts. Pippa wiped her eyes and looked at the horizon. Choppy green-grey waves raced towards the beach and hit the rocks in great explosions of foam, leaving ropes of stinking brown seaweed in their wake. The sulphur smell was so strong she could taste it in the back of her throat.

Pulling down her baseball cap, she pushed forward into the wind. 'I might spend my money in there,' she said, shouting to make herself heard and pointing towards the dark-blue building ahead. Jed saw the bookstore and pulled a face. 'You could go to the supermarket and meet me after?' she suggested.

He grinned. 'I'll get the food, no problem.'

'Great. Meet you back here when you're done.'

While Jed sprinted towards the supermarket, Pippa opened the grimy glass door to the bookstore. She'd looked around it once before, but didn't like how dark and chaotic it was. If anything, there seemed to be even more books crammed inside than last time. The sloping shelves sagged under the weight of musty old paperbacks and there were several stacks of oversized books in the middle of the floor that you had to edge your way around to get anywhere. Pippa preferred the bookshop at home where she met up with her friends on a Saturday. The books were brand new and there was a café that served milkshakes in tall glasses, and delicious blueberry muffins. This was a place where books came to die, and it smelled like it too.

It took her a while to spot anyone behind the dark wood counter. Not because there were lots of customers, but because she couldn't see around the towers of books. Ollie and a girl with long black hair were leaning forwards, reading a comic. The girl was wearing a fleecy blue-check shirt, the kind that Grandpa sometimes wore, and lots of silver necklaces. Pippa coughed but neither of them acknowledged her, which didn't seem the best way to greet a potential customer.

'Hi,' she said.

Ollie finally looked up and waved. 'Hi, Pippa! It's great to see you.' He glanced behind her. 'Where's Jed?'

'He's in the supermarket, getting some food for Grandpa.'

'Cool. This is Taylor, my cousin.'

'All right,' said Taylor, barely lifting her gaze.

She had the same brown skin as Ollie, but her face was covered with a smattering of freckles and framed by a heavy fringe. Pippa liked the way her black eyeliner flicked out at the sides. She'd tried to create a similar look at a sleepover party once, but it had come out wobbly. If she didn't have more urgent things on her mind, she might have asked Taylor how she managed to draw it so neatly. Her make-up made it hard to judge, but Pippa guessed she was fifteen, maybe sixteen at most.

'It's nice to meet you,' said Pippa.

Taylor popped a mouthful of bright-pink gum and turned the page of her comic.

Ollie shrugged. 'Don't mind Taylor. She's more into dead people.'

'Do you get many come in?' asked Pippa.

Taylor gave a tiny smile. 'Give it time.' Keeping her gaze on her comic, she pointed at the back of the store, where an elderly man wearing glasses was peering at a book.

Ollie wrapped an arm around his cousin, pulling her close. 'She's lovely once you get to know her. Honest.'

Taylor shoved him off and looked Pippa up and down. 'You from up-country, on holiday, like?' She couldn't have sounded any less interested if she tried.

'Yes.' Pippa didn't want to chit-chat either. She didn't know how long Jed would be, so she had to be quick. 'I was hoping you could help me with something, if that's OK?'

Pop went Taylor's gum.

Unsure whether that was a yes or no, Pippa continued. 'I've got these binoculars and I recorded something on them at night, but it hasn't come out. It happened once before, only I can't remember how I managed to view the footage.'

Taylor stuck out her hand and left it there. Pippa blinked, unsure what she wanted, then coughed to cover her embarrassment when she realised. Opening her rucksack, she took out the binoculars and handed them over.

'Proper job.' Taylor looked impressed as she turned the binoculars over in her hands. 'I've got the next model in the series. These ones have a decent enough range, but focusing is a pain. Whenever you use the manual focus, the view goes blurry while the auto-focus kicks in. If you're tracking something fast-moving you can forget it.'

Pippa nodded. She'd noticed this too.

'Did you set it to infrared before you hit record?' asked Taylor.

Pop went her gum.

'I'm not sure,' said Pippa.

Taylor smiled. 'If you recorded the video, it should still be there. You just need to select the same playback setting, yeah?'

Pippa sort of understood, but wasn't sure. 'Hopefully the video has been saved, but I don't know what folder it went into.' She pointed to the viewfinder, but Taylor had already opened up the clips and was looking through them. After five minutes of scrolling and repeatedly asking 'Is this the one?' and 'What about this?' she eventually found the file.

'Looks like you did record in infrared.' Taylor held out the binoculars for Pippa to see, then pointed to a dial on the side, which brought up a menu on the main screen. 'You just need to scroll through the playback settings – here, yeah – and select the right one. Then you should be able to see . . .' *Pop.* 'What was it you filmed again?'

Pippa's heart beat a little faster. 'A fox.'

'Right,' said Taylor, pressing the play button. 'So when you watch it back now you'll see the image is . . .' She peered at the screen. 'Is that an ancient stone site?'

'Can I have them back, please?' asked Pippa.

'Holy cow!' cried Taylor.

Pippa snatched the binoculars.

'What is it?' asked Ollie.

Before either of them could answer, the door opened and Jed came in. He was holding three carrier bags in one hand and a French stick in the other. He waved the bread in greeting then bit off a chunk from the end. Cheeks bulging, he chewed quickly and swallowed. 'Hi, I'm Jed,' he said to Taylor, stepping towards the counter with a smile. 'Pippa's brother. We're staying at my grandpa's place, down the lane from Ollie's house.'

'All right,' said Taylor, sounding not the least bit interested.

Pippa frowned at her brother in surprise. Jed was usually shy when he met new people. He stared at his feet and sometimes mumbled hello if he was feeling especially outgoing. What he *didn't* do was draw attention to himself by waving around foodstuffs or introducing himself to older girls with impressive make-up skills.

Ollie went over to him. 'Jed, bro! Give me a bite.'

Jed clutched the French stick like he was planning to use it as a weapon. Turning the bread on its side, he nibbled down the length of it the way you might eat corn on the cob. Ollie found this hilarious, and Taylor and Pippa shared a look that said *boy humour is weird*.

'That video,' whispered Taylor. 'It's legit, right?'

Pippa felt a thrill of anticipation run through her. 'Yes.'

Taylor leaned over the counter, her eyes wide with

excitement. 'Where did you film it? Was it a stone site round here?'

'Grandpa has an ancient stone in his garden,' said Jed through a mouthful of bread.

'His *garden*?' asked Taylor.

'It's not in his garden,' corrected Pippa. 'It's in a glade, between the garden and the forest.' As soon as the words had left her mouth, she wished she could have taken them back. Her only concern had been finding a way to make Jed and Dad believe her. She hadn't thought what would happen if others found out about the hidden folk.

Taylor jumped up and down. 'Can I see it again? Please?'

Pippa had no reason to distrust Taylor, yet she felt reluctant to hand over the binoculars. Realising it was too late to keep it a secret, she nodded then glanced at the boys. Jed had almost finished eating the French stick and was now unwrapping a family-size block of Cheddar. If she didn't stop him soon there wouldn't be any groceries left. 'You two,' she called. 'You need to see this.'

'A fox?' asked Ollie. 'Nah, you're all right. I've seen one before.'

Taylor grabbed him and dragged him over to look. 'Not like this you haven't!'

Jed stepped behind the counter too. The four of them crowded together and peered at the viewfinder while Taylor rewound the video and pressed play. The grainy black and white recording showed the stone, then the camera panned around to reveal tall wavering grass.

Ollie yawned, earning him a kick from Taylor.

Suddenly it was there, crouched at the edge of the glade: the same small creature with long hair and skinny arms and legs. Within its clawed hands was the mouse, desperately trying to escape. They watched in silence as the footage became shaky and the camera was lowered to the ground. And then the image returned and the camera zoomed in. The creature lifted up the struggling animal, broke its neck and then gulped at the air, seeming to swallow something before throwing the mouse to the ground. There was a snapping sound as Pippa stepped on a twig, and then the creature turned and looked straight into the camera. Its wings opened wide and it screamed.

After that, the images became blurry and began to jump. The binoculars must have continued recording as Pippa ran from the glade. She knew the creature had been gaining on her as she could hear the beating of its wings, but she had no idea it had come *that* close. Pressing pause, she stared at the freeze-frame image and felt sick. The creature's arm was reaching for her, its black clawed fingers touching her hair, its mouth open as if to bite.

'Is this a joke? One of those hoax things from the internet?' asked Ollie.

'It's real,' said Pippa. 'I filmed it at Grandpa's house.'

Ollie's face turned ashen. 'What *is* that thing?'

A feeling of dread crept over Pippa's skin. Seeing the creature again had taken her back to that night. She hadn't wanted to believe Grandpa when he said there were wicked things in the world, but it was true. Whatever that thing was, it had wanted to hurt her. 'I can only tell you what I've seen,' she said in a quiet voice. 'And what Grandpa told me.'

Taylor clapped her hands as if Christmas had come early. Ollie looked like he had a bad headache, and Jed was . . . Jed was eating a Cornish pasty. Pippa didn't get it. Even if he couldn't bring himself to apologise or admit that she was right, he could say *something*.

'The hidden folk are real, Jed.'

He wiped a lump of pastry from his chin and nodded.

'Aren't you going to say anything?'

'Yeah, I saw. Cool video.'

Pippa shook her head, deciding that she'd never understand her brother. Was he behaving like this to try and impress Ollie's cousin? Perhaps this is what thirteen-year-old boys did when they liked a girl: act all confident and eat too much.

'Come on, tell us everything!' Taylor insisted, jumping up to sit on the counter.

Pippa glanced around the shop, suddenly self-conscious. Reassured there were no customers close enough to hear, she told them about the twig men, and how her glass jars had been broken, and the voice she'd heard in her room telling her to stay away. She even told them about the woman she'd seen in the summer and Grandpa's story growing up.

The boys went off and stood by themselves. Even if he wasn't talking to her about the hidden folk and what they were going to do when Dad arrived, maybe it was good that Jed had a friend to chat things over with.

'I think your grandpa's right,' said Taylor. 'About it being hidden folk.'

Pippa felt a rush of fear and excitement. 'Do you know about them?'

'I've been researching them for ages, but I've never actually seen one.' Pulling open a drawer from the counter, she took out a folder and flicked through its pages. 'Hidden folk live at Neolithic sites. I've visited standing stones, caves, burial sites, you name it.'

'West Penwith is meant to have the highest

concentration of ancient stone sites in Europe,' Pippa told her. 'Like, hundreds of them.'

Taylor looked genuinely impressed, and Pippa felt herself warm to her. The older girl talked about her research and the places she'd visited, explaining that hidden folk don't show themselves to humans unless they want to be seen. As she listened, Pippa leafed through the folder. It was full of photos of empty warehouses, old houses and churches. Each file had the date and an observation report. Most were about ghosts, but there were other things too: vampires, poltergeists, demons, witches.

'Do you believe in *all* this stuff?' asked Pippa.

Taylor shrugged. 'Ghosts definitely; I've seen too much to doubt their existence. Other things, I'm not sure. That's why I do research and collect evidence.'

Pippa nodded. She didn't share Taylor's interest in the supernatural, but she recognised good scientific record-keeping when she saw it.

'Wait there a sec,' said Taylor. She ran to the back of the shop and returned with a battered-looking book called *Cornish Folklore & Otherworldly Beings*. 'It has a section about hidden folk. You might find it interesting.'

'Thanks. How much is it?'

'Don't worry. It's a gift.'

'Oh, are you sure? Thank you.'

'So what are you guys doing now?' asked Taylor.

Pippa was about to answer when a thud made her turn her head. Ollie had knocked over a pile of books in the middle of the store. Jed immediately dropped to his knees and began hastily picking them up, but when Ollie reached for a book and tried to help, Jed snatched it out of his hands. Pippa watched them for a moment, confused by her brother's reaction, then glanced back at Taylor. 'We're going to Grandpa's. Dad's on his way down.'

Taylor's face fell with disappointment. 'Can I come back with you? I want to see if I can pick up on the energies of the place and do a write-up for my file.'

Pippa bit her lip. 'Sorry, but I don't think Grandpa would like it.'

'You can't close the shop early,' interrupted Ollie. 'Mum is picking us up later, remember.'

'I thought these guys lived down the lane from you?' said Taylor. 'Get the bus with me now and I'll walk you home after. It'll be fine, Ollie Pops.' He started to complain, so she went over and held her hand across his mouth then turned her attention to Pippa.

'Please? If your grandpa doesn't want us there I promise we'll go straight away.'

Pippa didn't like to say no, especially as Taylor had been so kind. If it weren't for her, she wouldn't have the video to show Dad. 'I guess you could get the bus back with us. But you can't go anywhere near the glade.'

'You're a star!' said Taylor. 'You can trust me, I promise.'

Ollie broke away and gasped for breath. The look of alarm on his face told Pippa she was making a big mistake.

21

Ollie's cousin closed the shop and the children headed to the bus stop. Taylor wanted to know everything about the hidden folk and the stone, and barely waited for a response before asking something else. Pippa felt a little overwhelmed at first, but soon started to relax. It was a relief to tell someone what had been happening, and the more she talked the better she felt.

The bus arrived and the boys sat together behind the girls. Taylor asked Pippa about her grandfather and what her life was like at home. She wasn't just curious about the hidden folk; she seemed genuinely interested in Pippa as a person. When Pippa told her she'd asked for the binoculars because she wanted to shoot wildlife documentaries one day, Taylor said that sounded like the coolest job ever, second only to being a ghost hunter. It was nice to be listened to and taken seriously, and it reminded Pippa how she and

Jed had talked that way once. The realisation made her miss him, even though he was sitting right behind her.

The journey passed in a flash. As they got off the bus and walked towards Grandpa's house the children's mood changed. The dark fir trees loomed over them and an icy wind howled along the track, sending leaves and grit circling about their feet. The sky was filled with black rain clouds and the air had that electrically charged feeling you get before a storm.

Ollie had been to the house a few times before, but he looked afraid as he glanced around. 'I'm not sure this is a good idea,' he said, tugging on the sleeve of Taylor's red puffer jacket. 'Can't we just go back to mine?'

Taylor put her arm around his shoulder. 'Chill out, Ollie Pops. We won't stay long.' Pointing ahead, she shouted, 'Is that the glade?' Without waiting for an answer, she took out her phone and began to take photos.

'Yes, but you can't go in there,' warned Pippa.

Taylor ran over and took some shots through a gap in the bushes, her eyes wide with curiosity. Worried she might push her way through, Pippa went over and stood by her side. 'We should get inside the house.'

'Yeah, sorry,' said Taylor, then popped her gum.

Jed patted the broken oak tree. 'Hey, Newt, race you to the top!'

Pippa frowned. She'd love to climb the tree with him, but now was hardly the time. Jed had seen the video; he *knew* the hidden folk were real, so why was he acting like everything was normal? He must be trying to impress Taylor, though it seemed an odd way to go about it. Pippa felt the back of her neck prickle and glanced at the shed. There was no one there, but she had that same feeling of being watched again.

Unnerved, she hurried to the house and knocked on the door. After a few moments, the children heard bolts being drawn back and Grandpa appeared.

'You've brought friends here?' he asked in disbelief.

'It's OK,' said Pippa. 'They know about everything.'

Pippa had warned Ollie's cousin that her grandfather's hearing was bad. Taylor stepped forward and shouted, 'We won't stay long. I was hoping to look around and . . .'

Grandpa glanced behind them. Taylor started to say something else and he shook his head and ushered them inside. 'Don't just stand there!'

Taylor and Ollie entered first, followed by Jed and Pippa. Grandpa bolted the door and they made their way into the kitchen.

Raising her voice, Pippa tried to sound cheerful. 'You've met Ollie before. This is his cousin, Taylor. It's OK. They know about the stone and what's been happening.'

'Then you should know it's not safe here!' he complained. 'I brought you into the house because I didn't want you making a racket on the doorstep, but you can't stay. I'm sorry.'

Pippa's face flushed. Feeling awkward for her friends, she looked at Jed, hoping he might say something, but he was unpacking what was left of the groceries on to the kitchen counter. A half-eaten packet of cream crackers fell on its side and he quickly picked them up and stacked them in a pile. Pippa sat down, then opened her bag and pulled out the book Taylor had given her. Placing it on the table, she took out her binoculars and handed them to her grandfather. 'Taylor has been helping me with something. You need to see this.'

Grandpa took a seat next to her. 'What is it?'

Pippa rewound the video and pressed play.

He watched the flickering image, his expression changing from shock to revulsion. Pippa chewed her fingernail, waiting for him to say something. She paused the video at the moment the creature screamed and Grandpa peered at the screen, seemingly unable to believe what he was seeing. He turned and looked at his granddaughter as if he didn't recognise her.

'When did you take this?' he asked.

'Last night.' She sounded as wretched as she felt.

'Last night!'

'I'm sorry, Grandpa. I didn't mean to go into the glade. It was like I was sleep walking; I felt drawn there.' Even as she said the words she realised how weak they sounded.

'Why didn't you tell me before?'

Pippa squirmed in her seat. She should have, but she'd been putting it off because she knew how he would react. 'I couldn't get the video to play. Taylor helped me retrieve it.'

Grandpa rubbed his head. 'All the warnings I've given you, trying to keep you safe.'

'I'm sorry,' she said, fighting back tears.

Ollie gave her a sad smile as if he felt bad for her. Taylor had been reading *Cornish Folklore & Otherworldly Beings*, but stopped and nodded at her encouragingly.

'There's something else,' Pippa said to Grandpa. 'I went there in summer too and touched the stone, the day I had the bad dream and saw the woman.'

'You said you hadn't been near Whispering Hollow! I asked you that night!'

She wiped her eyes. 'I'm sorry. I didn't know anything bad was going to happen.'

Grandpa pulled her to him and stroked her head. 'Shush now, I'm sorry for shouting. This is all my fault. I should never have come back to this house.'

'Have you always known there was something here?' asked Taylor. 'I mean, have you seen the hidden folk yourself?'

Grandpa looked at her in surprise, as if he'd forgotten she was there. 'I knew something had been coming into the house, but . . .' His voice cracked and he shook his head, seemingly overwhelmed.

Pippa touched his hand. 'The woman visited me the same day I went to the glade. Maybe she came to warn me away from the stone, just like the man who visited you.'

Taylor pushed the book across the table towards them. It was open on a page with several ink drawings. 'The man and woman you saw, you said they were made from bark?'

Grandpa nodded.

Taylor tapped the page. 'Like this?'

Inside was a drawing of a person with their limbs made from branches. Sinewy vines twisted along their shoulders and tiny twigs sprouted from their arms and fingers. It didn't look exactly the same as the woman, but Pippa could see a definite resemblance.

She picked up the book and scanned a few paragraphs. According to the author, the beings were called spriggan and were faerie bodyguards. Grandpa peered over her shoulder as Pippa read aloud. 'In Cornish folklore, spriggan are guardians of the faerie realm. Notoriously bad-tempered, they take delight in playing cruel tricks on humans who offend them. If you steal faerie treasure or happen upon a hiding place, they will punish you. In the worst cases, they've been known to kidnap a human child and leave a changeling in their place.'

Pippa glanced across the room, surprised that Jed wasn't taking an interest in any of this. Even if he felt bad about not believing her before, surely he'd want to know what was living in the glade. Instead, he had his back to them, eating cream crackers. Pippa felt a twinge of unease. He'd had growth spurts in the past, but she'd never known him to eat *this* much.

While Grandpa sat at the table and flicked through the book, Pippa went over and stood next to Ollie. 'Have you noticed anything odd about Jed?' she said in a low voice.

'How do you mean?' he asked.

'You were talking to him in the bookshop and sat next to him on the bus. Does he seem different to you?'

'He's eating loads.'

Pippa nodded. It wasn't just that though. She couldn't put her finger on it, but he didn't seem himself.

Taylor leaned in and whispered, 'Why do you ask?'

Pippa stole a glance at Jed. 'He's usually shy when he meets new people, but he introduced himself to you in the shop and his face didn't twitch once.'

Taylor raised her eyebrows as if that didn't sound like much. 'When did it start?'

'Today, I guess, but he's changed a lot over the past few months.' Pippa couldn't bring herself to say that he'd been different with her ever since she'd started at the same school. The fact he didn't want to be seen with her was too painful. 'He doesn't want to play outside any more and he's always on his Switch or Xbox.'

Taylor shrugged. 'I used to love horses, but I haven't been riding in years. People like different things as they get older. Have you tried doing the things he enjoys?'

Pippa shook her head. He'd asked her to play Xbox with him lots of times, but she didn't like looking at a screen. Even if the weather was bad, she'd much rather be outside.

Grandpa lowered the book. 'What are you three whispering about?'

Pippa raised a finger to her lips and pointed at Jed, who had stopped eating and was now peering intently at something on the kitchen wall.

They watched as he picked up a large black spider. He let it run across his hand and then lifted his arm and brought it close to his face. For a moment, Pippa imagined he might eat it. Grandpa frowned. 'That's not like him.'

Pippa felt relieved and worried at the same time, pleased someone else had noticed Jed was acting differently, but afraid what it might mean.

'Wait a second,' said Pippa. 'I read something just now ... Can I?' she asked Grandpa, gesturing to the book. He handed it to her and she flicked through a few pages. 'There,' she said to the others, pointing to the bottom of a page.

Throughout history there have been reports of faeries abducting a human child and leaving an imposter in their place. These 'cuckoo' children typically look identical to those they have replaced and may retain some of their memories, yet they will exhibit

out-of-character or unusual behaviours. Common
indicators are an obsession with counting and a
voracious appetite.

Pippa laughed nervously and shook her head. 'I'm sure there's some logical explanation. It's probably just stress, or his hormones or something.'

She thought about the other things she'd read. The book said faeries punish humans who steal their treasure. When they were at the stone earlier, Jed had taken a piece of red glass. She'd thrown it back, but what if they'd decided to punish him? No. The idea was ridiculous. She'd grown up with Jed all her life. She'd know if it wasn't really him.

Grandpa stood up with a grunt and limped off towards the hallway. 'I'm going to phone your father. He should be here by now.'

Pippa nodded, but she wasn't really listening. Her mind was spinning with the possibility that the boy in the kitchen might not be her brother.

'Are you sure it's really him?' asked Taylor.

Pippa closed the book decisively. 'Yes.'

'OK, you know him best.' Taylor chewed her gum thoughtfully then lowered her voice. 'There's no harm in testing him though, right, just to be sure?'

Ollie glanced at his cousin. 'You said we wouldn't stay long.'

Ignoring him, she whispered excitedly, 'I've read about changelings. There are things you can do to find out.'

'Like what?' asked Pippa.

'People would throw them on a fire or push them into an oven. Or they'd try to trick them into revealing who they really are.'

Ollie winced. 'I vote for the last option.'

'Agreed,' said Pippa.

Taylor popped her gum. 'There was something about making them laugh. You had to serve them dinner in an egg shell. Changelings are meant to find it so amusing they jump up and declare their true identity.'

'Weird,' said Ollie.

Taylor nodded and continued. 'One was tricked into picking up some iron scissors. Iron burns them, apparently.'

'I read something about faeries not liking iron,' said Pippa.

'My mum keeps an iron horseshoe above the door in the kitchen,' said Ollie. 'She said it's to keep unwelcome things out.' He sighed. 'Can't we just ask a question only the real Jed would know?'

'I might have an idea,' said Pippa.

Taylor's eyes widened. 'What is it?'

Pippa took a quick breath to steady herself then went over to Jed.

'Doing you are what?' she asked.

He dropped the spider to the counter and spun round.

Pippa decided to try something easier. 'OK you are?'

Jed frowned at her, a confused expression on his face. 'OK am ... OK I ... OK.'

He stuttered over the words, repeating the phrase again. Pippa could tell he was trying to speak backwards, but it was like his brain didn't know how. She took a wary step back and smiled as if everything was fine, but inside her a dark hole was opening up.

Jed glanced at the others, seemingly aware they were staring at him. 'I'm not feeling very well. I think I need to lie down.'

Pippa couldn't leave things like this; she had to know one way or the other. Searching Jed's eyes, she lifted up his hand and brought it to his forehead. His expression remained the same: blank confusion. She pulled his hand away and tried again. His face didn't change. Realisation crept over her like a slimy film.

It wasn't him. It wasn't Jed.

Pippa released his arm and it dropped limply to his side. She shook her head, barely able to believe it was true. 'You're not my brother,' she said in a weak voice. 'You look like him, but you're not.'

The thing that wasn't Jed glared at her and then its eyes rolled back in its head. Stamping its feet in rage, it opened its mouth and let out a blood-curdling shriek.

22

Mamm peers out from the side of the shed and watches the children return to the house. There are others with them: a boy with short dark hair and an older girl with curious wide eyes. The boy tugs at the girl's arm, anxiety written across his face. He's right to be afraid. As soon as it gets dark, her masters will bring terror to this house and everyone inside it.

Mamm wonders if the newcomers are brother and sister. Spring Foot was always so headstrong, but there were times he looked at her that way. She pictures her brother standing in the courtroom, pleading at her with his eyes. Wrapping her arms around herself, she lets out a whimper.

'Oh, Spring Foot. I'm so sorry. I wish I could have saved you.'

Mamm's brother was everything to her. He was the safety of the ground beneath her feet and the thrill of a midnight storm. He was all things verdant, violent and quick and where he went he brought laughter, dance and song. Nothing was better than hearing him laugh. It rumbled inside his chest and came barrelling out of him like thunder. Mamm bangs her head against the shed, her heart chewed up with sadness. She will never hear him laugh again.

The youngsters have reached the house now. The two newcomers go inside first, followed by the red-haired children. Mamm turns away, not wanting to think about what's to come, not wanting to think about what she must do. The cruelty of it makes her breath catch. She knows better than anyone just how much it will hurt the girl.

23

The thing that wasn't Jed stopped shrieking and moved towards Pippa.

'Grandpa!' she yelled.

The changeling spun round and slammed the hallway door shut. Then it grabbed a chair and jammed it under the handle.

'What's happening in there?' shouted Grandpa from the other side.

'It's Jed!' cried Pippa. 'Only it's not him. He's blocked the door so you can't get in!'

'Open this door right now!' shouted Grandpa.

Ollie and Taylor went to Pippa's side. The three of them stood close together and stared about the room. The back door was boarded up and the windows were too small to climb through. They were trapped.

'What do we do?' wailed Ollie.

Grandpa shouted and tried the door handle. 'I mean it, let me in this instant!'

The changeling pressed both palms against the door and spoke in a cold voice. 'I'm sorry, Grandpa, but I can't let you in.'

Grandpa rattled the handle again. This time Not Jed screamed like a demon possessed, swearing and spitting out words of hate. Pippa covered her mouth and shrank back. Who knew what would happen if it turned on them? She had to do something – and fast.

'I've got an idea,' Pippa whispered to Taylor. 'There's a bag of pasta in the pantry. If I distract the changeling, can you open it and tip it on to the floor?'

Taylor frowned. 'Why?'

Pippa was about to explain when Not Jed glanced over his shoulder at them, as if sensing they were up to something.

Pippa's heart thumped as she stepped forward. She walked to the changeling's right, so that it turned its back to the pantry. 'Where's my brother?' she asked. Desperate to keep its attention on her, she raised her voice. 'What have you done with him? Tell me!'

Not Jed smiled earnestly and searched her face. 'What do you mean? You've known me all your life, you must recognise me.'

Pippa's breath caught in her throat. The boy standing before her looked and sounded so much like

Jed it was hard to believe it wasn't him. She *wanted* it to be him, and for this to have all been a terrible mistake. 'If you're him, prove it,' she demanded.

The changeling clutched her hand and its flesh was burning hot. She pulled away and Not Jed looked hurt. 'You asked me why I was upset about moving house, do you remember?'

Pippa swallowed hard.

'The truth is . . .'

A loud noise made the changeling pause and turn round. Taylor had opened the bag of pasta shells and was tipping them on to the pantry floor. She dashed out and the changeling ran over. Falling to its knees, it began scrabbling around on the tiles.

'Quick!' Pippa gestured to Ollie to pass her a chair. She closed the pantry door and lodged the chair under the handle. Then she ran to the table and frantically called for Taylor and Ollie to go to the other end. It was heavy, but they managed to carry it across the room. With the pantry door safely blocked, the children took a breath.

'How did you know to do the pasta thing?' asked Ollie.

'The book said they're obsessed with counting things,' replied Pippa. 'I remembered how weirdly the changeling reacted in the shop earlier, when you knocked over that stack of books. When we got back, it did the same thing, only it was counting crackers.'

Ollie's eyes widened, seemingly impressed.

'Talk to me, Pippa! What's happening in there?' shouted Grandpa.

She let him inside and threw her arms around his waist. He stroked her head and stared round the room. 'Will someone tell me what's going on? What's happened to Jed?'

BANG. BANG. BANG.

The pantry door jumped as the thing inside shrieked and threw itself against the wood.

'I guess it finished counting,' said Ollie.

Grandpa's face paled. 'What is that?'

Pippa bit the inside of her cheek. 'It's a changeling. It looks like Jed, but it's not him.'

'Let me out!' Not Jed shouted. 'You can't keep me in here!'

Grandpa's eyes were wild with worry. 'If that's not Jed, then where is he?'

Pippa couldn't answer. She didn't know if the hidden folk had taken him somewhere or done something to him. Thunder rumbled in the distance and rain lashed against the window. Imagining her brother frightened and alone in the dark was more than she could bear.

'When will Dad get here?' she asked.

'I don't know,' said Grandpa. 'I tried calling, but couldn't get through.'

Pippa's head pounded. The hidden folk came into the house at night, so they couldn't stay here. But they couldn't leave either – Grandpa couldn't walk far and she had to find Jed. 'Did you tell your parents where you were going?' she asked Ollie.

He shook his head.

Taylor took out her phone. 'No reception. I didn't tell anyone either.'

The children shared a worried look. No one was going to come looking for them.

'I could run to Ollie's and get help,' suggested Taylor.

'No,' said Grandpa firmly. 'It's getting dark. We'll stay put and wait for Pippa and Jed's dad to arrive. Though what he'll have to say about all this, heaven only knows.'

Taylor nodded. Despite her outwards bravado, Pippa thought she looked relieved.

Another crash of thunder sounded, this time right overhead. The lights flickered and went out, plunging the room into shadowy darkness.

'Let me out!' the changeling cried. 'I have to get out!'

Even though Pippa knew it wasn't really her brother trapped in the pantry, she couldn't help feeling sorry for the changeling. Jed had a fear of the dark and hated enclosed spaces. Years ago he'd had a panic attack while they were visiting some caves in Somerset. Seeing him shaking and gasping for breath had been frightening.

Grandpa went to the sideboard, picked up a box of matches and started lighting candles around the room.

'Please, Newt,' Not Jed sobbed. 'Please. I'm scared! I'm . . . I can't . . .'

'Just take deep breaths!' she called back. 'It's OK. You'll be OK.'

'Let me out!' the changeling whimpered.

It went quiet for a minute. Pippa held her breath and listened, wondering if it had passed out. BANG. BANG. BANG. She nearly jumped out of her skin as the hammering started again. It sounded different this time. Glancing at the others, she stepped back. 'I . . . I think it's using something sharp to get through.'

Everyone yelped as the wood splintered; fingers appeared through the gap, and then a single, staring eye.

'Please, Newt,' Not Jed panted. 'I know I haven't been very nice to you lately, but you don't know what I've been going through. Once I explain, you'll understand.' She started to walk away when the changeling called, 'It's about school!'

Pippa turned back. If the thing in the pantry had Jed's memories, maybe it really did know something.

'Go on,' she said.

'It's kind of private,' it whispered.

Pippa took a step closer to the table, which was acting as a barricade between herself and the pantry.

The changeling withdrew its fingers and peered at her through the hole. 'I don't want the others to hear. But if you come closer, I'll tell you.'

Pippa was about to climb on the table to get closer, when Taylor clutched her arm. 'If your brother wants you to know something about himself, he can tell you when we find him.'

Pippa felt her face flush. Taylor was right. If Jed really did have a secret he'd been keeping, then she'd rather hear it from him. The only thing that mattered was finding her brother. She turned to go and Not Jed shouted, 'Wait! You deserve to know the truth!'

A flash of lightning lit up the room and something darted by the window. Pippa turned and couldn't believe what she saw outside.

A twig man was prowling around the house. She could see its looped head and long arms and legs. It walked awkwardly, its limbs loose and dangling. How was that possible?

TAP. TAP. TAP.

A twig hand knocked against the window pane.

Ollie and Taylor cried out in fright.

The twig man walked past the window then stopped outside the back door. They could see its thin form through the glass, its hollow head moving as if it was searching for something. Pippa's heart pounded in her chest. How could it be alive? What did it want?

Grandpa tried to pull her away so she wouldn't see. She didn't want to look, but she had to know. A second twig man appeared behind the first, and then another. Before long a crowd of them were peering in through the windows and tapping on the glass.

24

Mamm wrings her hands as she paces the garden. The grey leaden sky presses down on her, the charge of electricity crackle-sharp in the air. It's not just the lightning storm she can sense coming. Her masters are preparing to attack. She can feel their cruel desire gnaw at her belly, taste the acidic fizz of their excitement on her tongue.

The house burns with light and she wonders what's happening inside. Has the girl realised the truth about her brother? Will they leave while there's still a chance for them?

Faster and faster she strides. The anticipation of what's to come fills her with such anguish she can't think straight. Determined to shake off her agitation, she turns and plunges into the forest. A brisk walk through the trees will clear her head.

She walks for ten minutes with no mind to where she's going, and then she sees something that makes her stop. A clump of fern shivers up ahead and then another. Whatever's moving through them must be invisible, which means only one thing. But why would her masters go into the forest; surely they'd want to attack the house?

The rumble of an engine sounds and a car appears, bumping along the dirt track with its headlights blazing. Mamm darts behind a tree and holds its trunk with both hands, willing it to hide her. Its branches creak and bend, wrapping her body tightly. Hidden from view, she watches the car draw level.

A bush at the side of the road shakes and one of her masters becomes visible and darts in front of the car.

The man grips the steering wheel, a look of sheer panic on his face. He swerves and there's a screech and a squelch of tyres as the car plummets into a ditch, leaving the back end raised high off the ground. Steam billows up into the cold night air and for a moment nothing makes a sound. Apart from the drip of water and fizz of steam the forest is quiet.

Mamm presses her back into the tree, her chest heaving. Why would one of her masters let themselves be seen, unless they wanted the vehicle to come off the road?

The man opens the car door and awkwardly slip-scrambles up the muddy bank. Running a hand over his bald head, he turns and peers into the gloomy trees. Then he fumbles in his coat pocket and pulls out something illuminated. 'Of course there's no reception!' he exclaims. 'That's what you get for living in a bloody forest!'

His breath comes in great white puffs as he walks around the car and mutters more things that make no sense to Mamm – about the madness of paying for the AA when he can't even call them, the stupidity of doing away with public phone boxes, and how it's uncivilised to live this far from an all-night convenience store.

Something rustles in the undergrowth and sinister laughter sounds.

The man spins round. 'Who's there?' He turns and looks in every direction. 'I know someone's there! Come out and show yourselves!'

He stumbles forward, shoved from behind by unseen hands. He just manages to straighten up when he's knocked off balance again and staggers to one side. More laughter sounds. Yelping, he clasps his hand to his leg, his trousers slashed by invisible claws.

'Why are they doing this?' Mamm wonders out loud to herself. They could easily take the man if they wanted, yet they choose to force him off the road and torment him.

To her surprise, a velvety voice answers. 'Not so clever, are you, spriggan?'

She startles and glances up into the branches of the tree. A crow with sleek black feathers stares down at her, its head turning this way and that.

'Are you . . . ?' she asks, already knowing the answer.

'Better than I was before,' it replies with a mean caw. 'You think you're being clever staying out of sight *caw*, don't you, spriggan? You think you can stay one step ahead of your masters, outwit them even? I don't know how this will end, but I know one thing *caw*. It will not end well for you.'

25

Not Jed shouted through the hole in the pantry door. 'I know what the twig men want. Let me out and I'll make them go away. I'm your brother, Newt. You can trust me!'

'Shut up!' yelled Pippa, clamping her hands over her ears. 'You're not my brother, so stop saying you are!'

Taylor held the book close to a candle. 'It's too dark, I can't see. Help me, would you, Ollie?' He opened it flat on the table while she took out her phone and turned on the torch. 'There must be something in here about them,' she said, desperately scanning the pages.

The twig men were jostling one another outside. Pippa couldn't be sure, but there seemed to be more of them than before. 'We need to barricade the windows!' she shouted, reaching for a chair before realising it was hopeless. There were too many windows and not enough furniture.

Taylor shut the book. 'I've checked the index and there's nothing. Tell me again what you know.'

Pippa took a deep breath. 'I think the hidden folk put the twig men inside the house as a warning not to trespass on the glade.' Suddenly a thought came to her. 'I was only able to see the hidden folk when I was using the binoculars. Maybe I should try looking through them now.' She grabbed them from the table and stepped towards the window.

'Careful,' warned Grandpa. 'Not too close.'

She lifted the binoculars to her face and gasped.

'What is it?' asked Taylor.

Pippa could barely believe what she was seeing. Dozens of creatures were flying in mid-air, some carrying a twig man by its arms and others holding a looped head in place. Working together, they made it seem like the figures were peering in through the windows.

'The hidden folk are moving the twig men so they look alive.'

'Like puppets, you mean?' asked Ollie.

Pippa nodded.

'But why?' asked Taylor.

Pippa couldn't answer. Maybe they were trying to frighten them, or perhaps there was some other reason. The truth was she didn't know what they wanted or what they might do. 'Maybe we should go to another room and hide.'

Not Jed called in a childish sing-song voice, 'Come out, come out, wherever you are!' He chuckled and then his tone turned nasty. 'They're going to find you. And when they do, you're not going to like it.'

A window smashed above the sink and a long twig arm poked through.

Grandpa startled and pulled the children close. 'We have to defend ourselves!'

'Hidden folk are afraid of iron and fire,' said Pippa.

'No!' exclaimed Grandpa. 'Fire's too dangerous.'

'Do you have anything made of iron?' Pippa asked.

Grandpa opened a cupboard. 'There should be some iron saucepans at the back there.' Pippa knelt down and pulled out the heavy pans while Grandpa opened a drawer and took out a pair of small gardening shears. Before long there was a pile of things on the counter. 'Quickly now,' said Grandpa, handing Pippa the shears, while the others each took a pan.

The twig man reached further through the window like it was trying to snatch at them and Pippa felt her tummy turn to water. The way it moved was so realistic she had to remind herself it wasn't actually alive.

'What if the iron doesn't work?' wailed Ollie.

Grandpa patted him on the shoulder. 'Then we'll think of something else. Come on. Stand with your backs together everyone!'

The four of them huddled close and looked around.

Pippa raised the binoculars and held her breath as she scanned the shadowy kitchen. Apart from the twig hand, nothing moved. Not Jed was quiet for once and the only sound was the howl of the wind and crack and boom of thunder. 'I can't see anything,' she whispered.

'Keep looking,' urged Ollie.

Pippa looked through them again. A movement in the corner of her eye caught her attention and she turned to the left. One of the hidden folk was flying outside the window. Gripped in its long pale fingers was a brick.

'Over there!' cried Pippa, pointing.

There was a sound of breaking glass as clawed fingers came through.

Taylor ran to the window, holding the pan before her. 'Where is it?'

'To your right!' shouted Pippa. 'No, your other right!'

Taylor swiped the air and there was a terrible shriek. For a split-second, the creature became visible. They could all see its pinched face, long silver hair and needle-sharp teeth. The skin on its arm sizzled as if it had been branded with a burning-hot poker.

Pippa had barely had time to draw breath when several more broke the glass panel of the back door and started tugging at the wooden boards nailed across it.

'The top of the door,' she shouted. 'No, wait ... the bottom!'

Grandpa jabbed with a pan and another one briefly became visible and screamed in pain, its leg badly burnt. A moment later it disappeared, just like the other one had. Looking through the binoculars, Pippa watched it crawl back outside and then scanned the room. The hidden folk were climbing through every window.

'Taylor, watch out!' she cried.

One squeezed through the broken window above the sink and jumped down on to the draining board, landing with a thud.

'It's next to the sink!' Pippa warned.

Suddenly they were everywhere. Taylor swung the iron pan at one but missed. It drew back like a cat and hissed, then leaped on to the floor and charged at Ollie. He tried to hit it, but it flew up and clawed his face, knocking his glasses and slashing him across the cheek. Taylor cursed as one bit her hand, making her drop the pan.

Another bounded towards Pippa. 'Grandpa, in front of you!' she cried.

He turned and swiped the air, stopping it from reaching her. 'Get away, you evil things!' he shouted. Enraged, it turned and wrapped itself around his leg, biting hard through his trousers. Grandpa gasped and Pippa watched helplessly as he stumbled and fell, hitting his head on the edge of the table.

'Leave him alone!' she yelled.

Something yanked her hair from behind. Yelping, she spun round and swung the iron shears, then ran to her grandfather and dropped to her knees. His head was bleeding and his eyes were closed. 'Grandpa, can you hear me?' she urged, shaking his shoulders. Tears welled in her eyes. 'Please, Grandpa, you have to wake up!'

Taylor and Ollie ran to her side. They knelt by her grandfather and swiped the air, doing their best to protect him. The hidden folk sniggered as they circled around them. Pippa expected them to double their attack while they were vulnerable on the floor, but they only scratched their hands and tugged at their clothes

'Grandpa?' she tried again. 'Can you hear me?'

He groaned and opened his eyes. 'What happened?' he asked.

Pippa pulled his arm and helped him to sit up. He glanced around as if he didn't know where he was, and then a look of alarm flashed into his eyes. 'Pippa! Are you OK? Are you hurt?' She shook her head and his face filled with relief. He tried to move and clutched his leg. 'My knee,' he said with a grimace.

'Just stay still,' pleaded Pippa. 'Don't move.'

BANG.

The back door flew open, letting in a blast of icy air. Pippa feared the hidden folk had broken it down, but it wasn't them she saw.

It was the strange tree woman she'd seen that night. Her limbs were made from branches and covered with lichen, vines twisting along her shoulders and neck. She had a dirty hessian sack for a head, with two holes cut out for eyes; attached to it were long knotty ropes that hung about her face like hair.

'What is it? What's there?' cried Taylor.

'A spriggan,' she whispered.

'Like in the book?' asked Ollie.

Pippa nodded. Only she didn't resemble the elegant tree figure in the drawing. She wasn't much taller than Pippa and looked like she'd crawled out from the earth. Thick warts covered her elbows and knees, the cankers clustered like angry dark blooms, and between her knuckles and toes sprouted tiny grey mushrooms. Her mouth was a split plum, ruby-red juices crusting at the corners of her lips. Worst of all were her eyes. A single acorn dangled in each of her empty eye sockets, swaying like a miniature bell.

'Can you see her?' asked Pippa.

'No,' said Ollie and Taylor at the same time.

Pippa pointed at the doorway and looked at Grandpa, but he shook his head. He couldn't see her either. She realised then that the hidden folk had stopped attacking and wondered if the spriggan had scared them away.

The spriggan walked forwards and a pungent stench rolled across the room, making the air taste green and wild. She smelled of the soil after it's been raining, and of rust, the sucked-penny tang of blood mixed with something bitter, herbs or the sticky sap of pine needles. Beneath it was a different smell: the sweet stink of fermenting fruit and musty decay. Although she didn't have real eyes, Pippa knew she could see her.

The spriggan beckoned to her and Pippa whispered, 'She wants me to go with her.'

'You can't!' said Taylor, grabbing her arm.

Not Jed called from the pantry. 'It's a trap, Pippa! Stay away from her! I know I'm not the same, but I still care about you. I don't want you to get hurt!'

Pippa hesitated. The fact the changeling warned her against going made her think she should. The spriggan had scared away the hidden folk, so maybe she was trying to help them.

The spriggan beckoned to her again then turned to go outside.

'Wait!' shouted Pippa. She squeezed her grandfather's hand. 'I'm going with her.'

Grandpa held on to her tightly. 'You mustn't!'

'You said the man who visited you was kind and felt like a friend. She might know where Jed is.'

'No, Pippa. You've always been such a fearless little thing, but it's too dangerous. You're to stay here and that's final.'

Pippa got to her feet.

Her grandfather's voice shook. 'Please, I can't lose you too.'

Seeing him so upset made her heart break. She didn't want to go against his wishes, but she needed to find Jed. 'I'm sorry, Grandpa. I'll be back as quick as I can.'

26

Pippa stood in the kitchen doorway and used her binoculars to check for hidden folk. Even though she couldn't see any, she didn't like the idea of going outside. What if they were lying in wait for her? There was nowhere to hide apart from the shed, and there was no way she'd be able to outrun them. She patted the iron shears in her pocket; at least she'd have some defence if they attacked her.

Steeling herself, she raised the hood of her coat and stepped outside. Rain pelted down at an angle, beating the sodden earth and lashing her face like a thousand tiny needles. The spriggan was already halfway down the garden. It was hard to see in the darkness, but there was something odd about the way she moved. Taking quick strides she jumped from side to side, her spindly legs and skittish movements like that of a spider.

'Wait!' called Pippa, hurrying to catch up. 'Where

are you going?' The wind snatched her words away and she raised her voice. 'Do you know where my brother is? Are you taking me to him?'

The spriggan paused at the entrance to the glade, then disappeared through the bushes.

Pippa's heart sank. It was the last place she wanted to go, but she'd come this far and wasn't about to turn back now. Stepping inside, she looked for Jed but there was no sign of him. There was only the stone shining grimly in the dim light and the spriggan, the ropes of her hair whipping about her head like angry dark snakes. She pointed at the hole behind her.

'You want me to go inside?' Pippa asked, astonished.

The spriggan's lips pulled back. It was hard to tell whether the expression was a smile or a grimace, but either way the effect was terrifying. What if she hadn't brought Pippa here to find Jed? What if this was a trap?

She shouldn't have come.

Pippa turned to go when the spriggan sprang forwards and grabbed her arm. She tried to pull free, but the twig fingers that gripped her were alarmingly strong and the more she struggled to escape the harder they dug into her flesh.

'Let me go!'

The spriggan spun her round to face her and Pippa's tummy did a somersault. The hessian sack of her head was mouldy and torn in places; ants and centipedes teemed in the dark hollows beneath it, her right cheek home to a mass of squirming white maggots. She leaned closer, her breath ripe with the smell of rotting flowers, and pointed at the stone.

'What's down there?' asked Pippa.

A clicking came from deep within the spriggan's chest and there was a faint rattling noise: a whirr, clack and wheeze. Her voice was like the wind through the trees, as dry and dead as winter. 'Your brother.'

'What? How?' exclaimed Pippa.

The spriggan didn't answer. She sat on the ground and lowered herself into the hole, dropping down so that her head was level with the earth. She held out her hand and there was something in the glint of her dark acorn eyes that seemed desperate, *hungry* even.

'My name is Mamm.' The spriggan tilted her head and Pippa had a feeling she was waiting for her to give her name in return. When she didn't speak, Mamm's shoulders dropped and she released a defeated-sounding sigh. 'You must come with me.'

Pippa swallowed her fear. She didn't want to follow the spriggan, but what choice did she have? If Jed was inside she couldn't leave him. Lowering herself into the hole, she found that she was standing in a cave. It wasn't pitch-dark as she'd expected, but filled with murky red light. There was no fire or candles and she couldn't understand where the light was coming from, until she noticed the walls were covered in spongy red moss giving off a peculiar crimson glow.

The cave was quiet, despite the storm outside, and Pippa had a sense that the world above had receded and was very far away. Peering into the gloom, she could just make out the opening of a tunnel. Mamm turned towards it and a low hissing sounded as she walked, each step releasing a waft of fungus spores and putrid vapour that rose about her head in a cloud, making Pippa think of a compost heap steaming with decay.

The tunnel was only just big enough to enter without having to duck her head and so narrow that Pippa couldn't stretch out her arms. The red glow was dimmer here and she could barely make out the shape of Mamm's back as she hurried away. Sinewy tree roots covered the walls and poked out of the earth like bony fingers, scratching at her face and snatching her coat, the ground so uneven that several times she tripped and almost fell.

Pippa had a feeling she was being watched, but whenever she turned around she couldn't see anything. At one point she thought she saw a face in the wall of the tunnel, appearing and reappearing in the earth. When she looked closer, the face vanished. Several times she heard laughter, but it was always on the edge of her hearing and she could never figure out where it was coming from.

They passed a dozen tunnel openings and chambers as they walked, some large and others narrow and choked with dangling tree roots. How big *was* this place? It made Pippa's mind spin to think there was an entire other world beneath the ground, one which humans knew absolutely nothing about. They turned down a narrow opening and Pippa gasped as a black spider the size of her hand scuttled over the ground. It had eight hairy legs, but instead of a body there was an eyeball. It blinked at her – blinked! – before scuttling away.

They turned down another passageway and Pippa spotted a group of pale mushrooms clustered on the ground. They had long thin stalks with rounded grey caps, the undersides textured with frills and folds. Although there was no wind, they swayed from side to side. She bent down to inspect one, and it jumped into the air and floated upwards. What she'd thought was a stalk was actually a tiny person. A squashed, wrinkly face glared at her then grabbed the domed cap on its head and pulled it down to hide itself from view.

Pippa had barely had time to react, when tens of glowing green cockroaches teemed down the wall next to her. They made a hissing noise that sounded like *trespasser* as they hurried by, then disappeared into a hole in the earth. She walked on and startled as something hopped across her path: a warty toad whose skin was covered with tiny mouths that opened and closed. She stared at it, repulsed and yet fascinated. How could such things exist?

Perhaps she was dreaming and the past few days had never happened. She'd decided that any moment now she would wake up, when Mamm stopped by the entrance to a cave. 'Don't try to free him,' she warned. 'It will only hurt more.'

'What?' cried Pippa.

She rushed inside and halted in shock. Her brother was standing at the back of the cave, his body pinned to the wall by a mass of twisted tree roots.

'Jed!'

Her initial relief at seeing him quickly turned to horror. His eyes were closed and she couldn't tell if he was breathing or not. Dirt covered his face and tiny rootlets had forced their way into his mouth as if they were growing inside of him. She ran to him and desperately pulled at one of the roots around his leg. As soon as she touched it, new tendrils lashed out and whipped about his thigh, cutting through his jeans and slicing into his flesh. Pippa flinched as if her own body had been cut.

'What's happening?' she demanded. 'Let him go!'

Mamm drew herself up to her full height. 'My masters have decided to punish you for trespassing on their home. They were listening when you made a wish upon the stone and have drawn upon your heart's desire to create your perfect brother. The boy you see now will remain here, and the changeling will take his place.'

Pippa covered her mouth, appalled as she remembered the words she'd thrown at Jed in a rage that morning: *I wish I had a different brother.*

Mamm continued, 'If your new brother isn't to your liking, he can easily be changed. In time, no one will notice the difference.'

Pippa touched Jed's shoulder. Even though she wished he was nicer to her sometimes, she wouldn't change him for the world. She didn't care if he was moody and didn't talk to her in school; she didn't care if he never played with her again.

'I want to talk to your masters.'

'No,' said the spriggan.

'There must be something . . .' Pippa's voice cracked as a wave of despair washed over her. The thought of Jed spending the rest of his days underground was too awful to think about. 'Can't you help us, please?'

Mamm started to turn away.

Pippa looked at Jed and felt a surge of love so strong she knew she'd do anything for him.

'What if I stayed here instead of him?'

Mamm turned back, seemingly caught off balance. 'My masters are cruel, they would torment you and . . .'

Pippa covered her ears. 'I don't care! Just let my brother go!'

Mamm wrung her hands and paced back and forth. 'I can't,' she murmured. 'If I don't do as they say they'll send me to ground for good. It will not end well for me.'

Pippa listened with interest. If Mamm was afraid of the hidden folk, maybe they could join forces against them. 'These masters of yours . . . if we worked together, could we stop them?'

Mamm laughed bitterly and shook her head. 'They can kill me just like that,' she said, clicking her twig fingers. She crossed the cave and gazed at Jed, seemingly deep in thought.

'There must be a way to help him,' insisted Pippa. 'I can't leave him here.'

Mamm nodded as if she understood how Pippa felt. When she spoke, her voice was a choked whisper. 'I had a brother once. His name was Spring Foot.'

'What happened to him?' asked Pippa.

'My masters killed him.' She let out a long sigh as if she'd endured more loss than she could put into words. 'I used to have many brothers and sisters, but they've all gone now. I'm the last of my kind.'

Pippa wondered why her masters had killed Spring Foot and what had happened to her other siblings, but it didn't feel right to ask. Part of her didn't *want* to know about the hidden folk and the cruel things they'd done. 'I'm sorry,' said Pippa. She meant it too. The thought of losing Jed was terrible and she couldn't imagine how it must feel to be all alone in the world. She reached out and touched Mamm's arm. 'I wish I could help you.'

Mamm startled and stared at Pippa's hand as if she hadn't been touched for a very long time. 'Why?' she asked in a timid voice.

'You're not like the hidden folk,' said Pippa. 'They're full of hate and I can tell how much you loved Spring Foot and the others.' Mamm didn't respond and Pippa continued. 'My grandpa told me how he met a spriggan when he was a boy. He climbed through his bedroom window one night. Grandpa said he had a big mossy beard and bushy green feet, and when he laughed it was the most wonderful sound. He said he was kind. I think you might be kind too.'

Mamm turned to her in surprise, and Pippa felt she might have said something important.

'Spring Foot told me he'd made friends with a boy in the forest. He said they'd talked for hours and would chuckle whenever he spoke of the child; I could tell he was fond of him.' She looked sad for a moment and then seemed to gather herself. 'Perhaps there is a way . . .' Gently stroking Jed's hair, she looked around the cave. 'But we have to be quick. I don't know if they're watching.'

The spriggan reached out and touched one of the roots across Jed's chest. It shrank back and Pippa blinked in amazement as the roots around his arms and legs dropped to the ground. The tiny rootlets in his mouth fell away and he coughed and spluttered.

'Jed!' cried Pippa. 'It's OK, I'm here.'

His eyelids fluttered open. 'Newt,' he slurred. 'You came for me.' His head lolled to one side and he slumped against the cave wall and closed his eyes again.

A tear of relief rolled down Pippa's cheek. Mamm placed an arm round her and she wiped her face and managed a tiny smile.

They started to pull Jed away from the cave wall when the air shimmered.

One of the hidden folk appeared from nowhere. Like the others it had a furry, rabbit-like face and leathery wings, but its long straggly hair was black rather than silver and instead of rags it wore a suit, with chains of tiny human teeth around its neck.

Mamm lowered her eyes. 'Badnerjak, please. I can explain . . .'

Badnerjak hissed at her, and then stepped towards Pippa. His forehead wrinkled as he sneered, whiskers twitching. 'We warned you to stay away, trespasser. You didn't, so now you'll pay.'

'I'm sorry, I didn't mean to . . . We'll never go near the stone again,' she promised. 'Just let my brother go.'

'Let him go?' Badnerjak laughed.

Pippa stiffened. 'What are you going to do?'

Badnerjak turned on Mamm. 'You haven't shown her?'

Oily green fluid leaked from Mamm's eyes and trickled down her cheek as she turned to Pippa. 'I hoped you wouldn't see—'

Badnerjak struck Mamm across the face. 'Don't think your betrayal will go unpunished, spriggan!'

'See what?' asked Pippa.

Mamm's arm shook as she pointed further back into the darkness of the cave.

Pippa peered into the gloom. A shadowy figure was sitting against the cave wall, its body held by tree roots and its face covered with leaves. 'Who is it?' she asked.

'Take a look,' said Badnerjak.

Pippa didn't want to go near it, but she had to know. What if they'd managed to abduct Taylor or Ollie? What if it was Grandpa? She walked forwards and pushed aside one of the thick leafy branches. The face beneath was covered with a slimy film that stuck to her fingers. She pulled her hand away and the translucent membrane came away with it.

'N-no,' she stammered.

'Rather a good likeness, don't you think?' asked Badnerjak.

Pippa studied her own face, unable to speak. It felt as if she was looking into a mirror, except her eyes were closed. The changeling's long auburn hair was messy like hers, and it had the same rosebud mouth and snubbed nose covered with freckles. Unlike her, it wasn't breathing. The stillness was eerie – it was like seeing herself sleeping, or dead.

Pippa took several steps back. Badnerjak raised his right arm and a rush of air slammed into her body, knocking her off her feet. She thumped into the cave wall, so that she was slumped next to the changeling.

Seeing it so close made her stomach turn. It had a mole under its right eye, just like she did, and a tiny scar above its left eyebrow where she'd fallen off her bike last summer. The back of her neck began to sweat as cold realisation washed over her. The changeling was going to walk out of the cave and carry on with her life, while she remained trapped down here with Jed forever.

'You can't do this!' she shouted.

A tree root twisted around her ankle and another snaked across her thigh.

Fear turned to anger and she kicked her feet and screamed. 'Let me go!'

Badnerjak leaned close. His breath was rank and Pippa turned her head away. She didn't want to cry, but the thought of never seeing Grandpa or Mum and Dad again was too much and she let out a sob.

'Shush now, there's no need to get upset,' said Badnerjak, stroking her hair. 'You won't feel a thing.' Smiling, he plucked a hair from her head.

Pippa winced. 'What are you doing?'

Badnerjak placed the strand of long auburn hair on to the changeling's head. Then he prised open its mouth.

'Wait!' yelled Pippa. Roots slithered around her legs and one crept across her tummy. She gasped as it

215

tightened. 'There must be a deal we can do . . .' she panted. 'A trade!'

Badnerjak's head snapped towards her. 'What do *you* have to trade?'

Pippa racked her brains, trying to think of something. She remembered how the hidden folk punished those who stole their treasure. 'I have a ruby in my pocket,' she blurted. 'There's more hidden in the house. Let us go, and I'll trade them for our lives.'

Badnerjak sniffed and twitched his nose. 'Show me.'

Pippa wriggled her arm beneath the root that was holding her then stopped. 'I can't reach it,' she lied.

Grunting with impatience, Badnerjak plunged his hand into her pocket. He screamed and pulled back his arm, letting the iron shears drop to the ground. His palm sizzled and a smell of burning flesh filled the air as he collapsed to his knees.

Pippa desperately tugged at the thick tree root wrapped around her middle. Instead of loosening it grew tighter, almost crushing her.

'Help me!' she gasped.

Mamm rushed forward and grabbed the gnarled root with both hands. She frowned in concentration and it shrank back.

Pippa watched Badnerjak writhing on the ground in

216

agony. How long until he noticed she was escaping? What if more hidden folk came?

'My arm,' urged Pippa.

Mamm grasped the root that was pinning her upper body, and it fell away. Able to move more freely, Pippa pulled at a root holding her leg, snapping it in two.

Badnerjak looked up and hissed, 'You'll pay for this, trespasser!'

Breaking free of her binds, Pippa stood then picked up the shears and returned them to her pocket. Working together, she and Mamm pulled Jed from the cave wall.

'Get back here!' yelled Badnerjak, awkwardly getting to his feet.

Mamm shouldered more of Jed's weight. 'Quickly!' she cried. 'Run!'

Badnerjak started after them, then stumbled into the cave wall and clutched his arm.

Pippa's heart hammered in her chest. Too scared to check if they were being chased, she ran down the tunnel. Jed's eyes were shut and his head lolled to one side as they dragged him along. Pippa was glad. She didn't want him to realise where he was and be afraid. 'It's going to be OK, Jed,' she whispered through snatched breaths. 'We're going to get you out of here.'

27

They returned to the entrance cave and lowered Jed to the ground, where he lay curled up with his eyes closed. Pippa checked the tunnel behind her, but there was no sign of Badnerjak.

Mamm seemed to read her thoughts. 'They'll send more than one next time,' she warned. 'My masters are arrogant – they never believed a human could outwit them, especially not a human child. But they won't make the same mistake again.'

Pippa's breath caught. 'How many of them are there?'

'Fifty, maybe more. I imagine they'll be at the house now, tormenting the others inside.'

'Why?'

'They wish to punish you for trespassing.'

'But why attack the others? They haven't done anything!'

Mamm tilted her head as if considering the

question. 'Hurting those you love is a way to hurt you. My masters enjoy seeing the fear in their victims' eyes. It pleases them.'

Pippa shuddered. When Grandpa had fallen and they were huddled together on the kitchen floor, the hidden folk had laughed as they'd circled around them, clawing their arms and faces. They'd enjoyed frightening them. If they were punishing her for trespassing on their home, what would they do now that she'd injured Badnerjak? She had to be ready. 'What if I used fire against them?'

Mamm flinched. 'They fear fire the most.'

'I could trap them,' said Pippa, thinking out loud. A plan was forming in her head, but she didn't know if it would work. 'How can I make them come to the stone?'

'They'll defend their home if it's under attack.'

Pippa stuck out her chin. 'That's it,' she said. 'I'll threaten the stone with fire. When the hidden folk come, I'll force them underground and trap them inside.'

'It might work,' said Mamm. 'But it won't be easy.'

Pippa nodded. It was a relief to have an ally, yet so many things didn't make sense. 'If they're your masters, why did they leave when you entered the house?' she asked.

'They wanted you to think I'd frightened them away. That way you would trust me and follow me to find your brother.'

Pippa clenched her fists. 'Who took Jed?'

'I took him.' Pippa recoiled and Mamm added quietly, 'I did as my masters instructed. I dragged him into the stone and they took a hair from his head and brought his changeling to life.' Though she hadn't apologised, the slump of her shoulders suggested she regretted her actions. She squatted down and looked at Jed. 'Your brother is lucky to have you. I wish I'd been able to help mine when he needed me.' Her voice faltered and she took a shaky breath. 'Cherish him – always.'

'What will you do now?' asked Pippa.

'I'll go to the place I buried Spring Foot. I'd like to be with him when my time comes.'

'Is there no way you can escape?' asked Pippa. 'Is there really nothing we can do?'

Mamm laid her hand on Pippa's arm. 'I am old and have lived many years. It's time I let the ground have me.' With that, she took several steps back. 'Go now, I will guard the tunnel in case Badnerjak appears. I can slow him down if nothing else.'

Pippa squeezed Mamm's hand and smiled sadly, wishing they had more time. Then she knelt down by

Jed. 'Can you hear me?' She shook him and he opened his eyes. 'I know you're tired, but we have to go.'

'Where are we?' he asked groggily.

'Under the stone.'

'How did we get here?'

'You need to hold on to the earth and pull yourself up,' said Pippa.

He got to his feet and scrambled up the bank. Pippa followed after him and inhaled the cold night air, relieved to be above ground. The blustery wind had dropped and it was no longer raining, the storm now passed.

Jed flicked his hair from his eyes. 'It's dark. Why's it dark?' When Pippa didn't answer, he stared about the glade. 'The last thing I remember it was morning and we were arguing. You walked off and I was by the stone. And then something hit my head and I was knocked off my feet.' His cheek twitched and he added in a whisper, 'I remember being dragged across the grass, then I must have passed out.'

Pippa put her arm around his shoulders, hating the thought of him being frightened and alone. 'It's OK,' she said. 'You're safe now. But we have to stop the hidden folk from attacking the house.'

'What?' He searched her face in alarm. 'Is Grandpa OK?'

Pippa felt a lump rise to her throat. She had no idea whether their grandfather and the others were safe or what might be happening to them. Taking Jed's hand, she pulled him out of the glade. 'I'll tell you everything, I promise, but we need to hurry.'

He yanked away from her grasp. 'Where are we going?'

'To the shed.'

'Why?'

'Please, Jed. I know none of this makes sense to you and it must be really scary, but you have to trust me.'

He stopped and held her gaze. The fear and confusion on his face lifted and a look of certainty entered his eyes. 'I'm sorry I didn't believe you before.'

Pippa shrugged as if it didn't matter, but his words meant everything to her. 'It's OK. I wouldn't have believed me either. But we have to work together now.'

Jed gave her a brief hug and then they hurried across the garden. Pippa opened the shed and searched the racks of tools and boxes on the floor. There had to be something she could use. 'We'll need something long, a pole of some kind,' she said. A quick scan of the shelves didn't reveal anything, and then Jed pointed to a broom propped against one wall.

'Would that do?' he asked.

'Yes!' said Pippa. She pocketed some matches from the shelf, then unscrewed the lid of the petrol can and poured the liquid over a pile of rags before tying them round the bottom of the broom. 'We're going to need some wood too,' she said. Jed went over to a pile of logs and picked up as many as he could carry, then dropped them into the wheelbarrow by the compost heap. Pippa poured petrol over the wood, noticing the large plastic water butts Grandpa used to collect rainwater. If something caught fire that shouldn't, it was good to know they were there.

They returned to the glade and Pippa used her binoculars, relieved to see it was empty. 'Throw the logs down there,' she said, pointing at the hole.

Jed did as she instructed then wiped his hands on his jeans. 'Do you want me to light it?'

'Not yet,' said Pippa. 'First we need to set the broom alight. The hidden folk will come to defend their home and I have to force them into the stone.'

'How?' asked Jed, looking panicked.

'They're scared of fire.' She handed him the binoculars. 'You'll need these to see them. Tell me where they are, and stay close to me.'

Jed's cheek twitched, making him squint. 'It sounds dangerous, Newt. Are you sure you know what you're doing?'

Pippa nodded. Temporarily trapping the hidden folk was their best chance; she just had to hope all of them went underground before she started the bonfire. She took the box of matches from her pocket. 'I don't know how long it will take for the fire to burn down – an hour or two maybe – but it should give us time to cycle to Ollie's house and get help.'

Jed nodded grimly and Pippa struck a match. She threw it on the petrol-soaked broom and it went up with a whoosh. Gritting her teeth, she advanced towards the stone and shoved the burning end into the hole.

'What do you see?' she asked.

Jed scanned the clearing with the binoculars. 'Nothing ... There's nothing.' A minute passed and then he gasped. 'Wait. I think ... Oh my God, Newt! They're coming!'

'How many?'

'I – I don't know. Thirty, forty maybe. They're flying this way.'

Suddenly they were upon them. 'Tell me where, Jed!'

'Right in front of you!'

Pippa lunged with the broom and there was a sickening screech as one of the hidden folk flashed visible, the tips of its wings on fire.

'To your left!' shouted Jed.

Pippa jabbed with the broom, but missed.

Jed yelped and clasped his arm. The back of his hand was badly clawed.

Shaking with rage, Pippa swung the broom. There was a shriek as another one briefly became visible, and then another. High-pitched screaming filled the air, making the children's ears ring. It wasn't the sound of a rallying war cry, but one of panic.

Pippa continued to swipe the air with the burning broom. After a few minutes, she realised they hadn't heard a single shriek and none of the hidden folk had clawed them.

Jed looked through the binoculars. 'It's working!' he shouted. 'They've gone inside.'

'All of them?' asked Pippa.

'Yes, I think so.'

She lowered the broom and spoke under her breath, almost not daring to believe it was true. 'It worked. It actually worked.' All they had to do now was light the bonfire and the hidden folk would be trapped inside the earth. Smiling, she ran towards Jed.

'We did it!'

A blow to the back of her legs brought her to her knees.

'Ow!'

The broom fell from her hands and landed on the

grass. She went to pick it up, but it wouldn't budge. And then she realised why. Badnerjak was standing on the handle. She tried to get to her feet, but he shoved her to her knees.

'Leave my sister alone!' Jed ran over to them, his face pale with shock.

Badnerjak raised his arms. 'Please, you misunderstand.' His whiskers trembled as he shook his head. 'I mean no harm!' He showed his palms in a gesture of surrender and Pippa noticed one of his hands was bandaged with a dirty white cloth.

She got to her feet. 'Don't listen, Jed!' she yelled, but he was staring wide-eyed at something behind her.

Pippa glanced over her shoulder and her body turned to ice. It was her changeling, but this time it was awake – and walking.

The changeling went to her brother and hugged him tight. 'Jed, thank God!' it cried. 'You're alive!'

Jed's mouth hung open. 'W-what?' he stammered. 'How can . . . ? I don't . . .'

'It's me, your sister,' insisted the changeling. 'You've been talking to an imposter. Thank goodness you got away from her; who knows what might have happened otherwise.'

Pippa stared in disbelief. Meeting an identical version of herself in the cave had been awful, but to

227

see it living and breathing . . . She tried to warn her brother but the words stuck in her throat. 'Jed, don't listen!' she eventually managed. '*I'm* your sister.'

Jed's face went grey and clammy as if he might throw up. 'This can't be happening,' he said, glancing from one girl to the other. 'I'm dreaming . . . or hallucinating or . . . or something!'

The changeling took hold of Jed's hand. 'I'll explain everything once we get inside the house. The hidden folk aren't bad. That was *her* making up stories and trying to scare you. Come on. Let's go before she tells you any more lies.'

Pippa rushed forward, unable to hide her panic. 'It's not true, Jed! The girl standing next to you is a changeling! The hidden folk made her and brought her to life. They attacked the house and were going to keep us both trapped underground, but we escaped. Don't you remember walking through the tunnels?'

He took an uncertain step back. 'I remember waking up and you telling me to climb.'

Badnerjak walked over to them and snorted. 'I'm afraid you've been fooled by that imposter,' he said, pointing at Pippa. 'My kind are peaceful, we haven't attacked anyone. This changeling hit you on the head and dragged you into the stone. When you woke up, she only pretended she was helping you.'

Jed tugged his hair with both hands. 'This is insane.' His breath came fast and shallow. 'Hidden folk, changelings . . . It's not . . . I can't . . .'

Not Pippa put its hand on his back. 'It's OK. Breathe, you need to breathe. Like Dad showed you on holiday in Somerset, remember?'

Pippa watched in dismay as Jed's eyes filled with recognition, seemingly convinced he was talking to his sister. And then the changeling did something that was utterly terrifying. It held Pippa's gaze and smiled. She recognised the look because it was one she used herself. It said, *I've won and there's nothing you can do about it.*

'How did she get here?' asked Jed, stealing a wary glance at Pippa. 'Is she a clone or something? Who made her?'

'A witch who dwells in the forest used bad magic,' Badnerjak confided in a whisper. He glanced around, seemingly afraid of being overheard. 'She created the changeling and sent it to kill you.'

Pippa felt the blood drain from her face. 'No! That's not true!'

'My sister said she saw a strange woman on her windowsill last summer,' said Jed.

'That was the witch!' exclaimed Badnerjak. 'Now do you believe us?'

Pippa lunged towards Jed. 'Please, can't you tell it's me?'

'Stay away from us!' cried the changeling. It hugged Jed around the neck and Pippa's heart sank as her brother patted it on the shoulder.

'Don't worry; I won't let it hurt you,' he soothed. The changeling pulled him away by the arm.

'No!' sobbed Pippa. 'You can't go . . .'

'Quiet!' ordered Badnerjak. He kicked her legs from beneath her and she landed on her knees. Grabbing her round the throat, he sneered and licked his lips. 'Not so clever now, are you, trespasser?'

Pippa turned her head, but couldn't get free.

Breathe, she had to breathe.

Clutching Badnerjak's fingers, she tried to prise them away but she wasn't strong enough. She looked to Jed for help, but he had his back to her, heading towards the house. At one point, he started to look over his shoulder, but the changeling stopped him. Dimness clouded Pippa's vision, the pressure in her head unbearable. Fuelled by panic, she grabbed Badnerjak's injured hand and dug her fingers into his palm. He yowled and she broke free.

'Wait!' she gasped. 'I can prove it's me!'

Jed stopped and turned around.

Pippa took a ragged breath and staggered over to

him. If the changeling had her memories, asking it questions only she would know wouldn't work. She stood before her double and studied its face. The likeness was unnerving. 'I can prove it's a changeling,' she insisted. 'I just need time!'

The changeling bared its teeth as if it wanted to bite her, its expression one of pure hatred. Pippa remembered the way Not Jed had screamed when it realised she knew it wasn't her brother, and it gave her an idea. Leaning close, she looked the changeling in the eye. 'You're a fake! Your hair isn't the same colour as mine and the way you walk is all wrong.' Pippa shoved its shoulder. 'You're a fake! A stupid, rubbish fake!'

The changeling's eyes rolled back in its head and then its whole body shook. Its arms jerked violently as it stamped its feet and shrieked like a thing possessed. There could be no mistake – whatever it was, it wasn't human.

Jed stepped back and stared in shock, and Pippa lunged into action. Picking up the burning broom, she held it towards Badnerjak and set fire to his hair. The flames crackled and leapt and an acrid burning smell filled the air. Howling, he fled into the stone.

'No!' the changeling screeched. 'No! No! No!'

It came towards Pippa, its face twisted with rage.

Pippa jabbed with the broom and a spark of flame landed on the changeling's coat. It went out almost instantly, but the changeling panicked as if it had been set on fire. Screaming, it turned and ran after Badnerjak, following him into the stone.

Jed rushed to his sister. 'Are you OK? I'm so sorry . . . Oh, Newt!'

Pippa wiped her eyes. 'Are the hidden folk all inside now – can you check?'

He picked up the binoculars hanging round his neck and looked in every direction. 'I can't see any left.'

'You're sure?'

He looked again. 'Yes.'

Pippa stepped forward and winced.

'Are you OK?' asked Jed.

'My ankle, I twisted it.'

Jed held the burning broom in one hand and put his other arm round his sister. Together they approached the stone. 'I need to light it,' said Pippa.

Jed handed her the broom and she lowered it on to the pile of wood. After a few moments it caught flame, sending a waft of thick smoke into the stone. Hopefully, it would give them enough time to get help.

Shouts of alarm sounded inside. Pippa paused to stare at the dark hole and felt relieved and guilty at

232

the same time. She didn't want to hurt the peculiar animals she'd seen and hoped they'd be all right.

The children walked back to the house in silence, too shaken and exhausted to speak. They were halfway across the garden when Pippa stopped.

'What is it?' asked Jed. 'Do you need to rest?'

She searched the shadowy darkness, her gaze lingering on the base of the broken oak tree. 'No, I'm fine. I thought I saw . . . It's nothing.'

Jed jogged up the drive and tried the front door, but it was locked.

'Let's go round the back,' said Pippa.

He helped her hobble around the side of the house. Bits of twig men were strewn across the gravel pathway as if an army of them had been cut down. 'Look, Newt!' cried Jed, pointing at the back door. It was hanging off its hinges, the glass smashed.

Pippa took his arm from around her and rushed inside, her ankle forgotten. 'Grandpa, where are you? Grandpa!'

28

The kitchen resembled a war zone. The floor was covered with broken crockery and glass from the windows, and several chairs had been knocked over. Pippa peered around. It was so quiet it felt as if the house had been abandoned.

'Grandpa, are you there?' called Jed.

His voice was swallowed up by the darkness. The children strained to listen as they crossed the room, but the only sound was the angry crunch of glass under their trainers.

'Grandpa!' Pippa shouted desperately. They were about to open the hallway door when a voice whispered from the other side.

'Pippa? Jed? Is that you?'

Jed turned to his sister in surprise. 'What's Ollie doing here?'

The door creaked open and Ollie and Taylor appeared, both of them brandishing a saucepan. They looked tired and shaken up, their hands and faces covered with scratches. Taylor lowered her weapon and hugged Pippa. 'You're OK!' She pointed at the room behind her. 'After you left, we hid in the living room and barricaded the windows and door. The hidden folk came back, but we managed to keep them out. Then it all went quiet, and . . .'

Taylor paused to draw breath and Ollie took over. 'We heard Jed but we didn't know if it was him, so we stayed put.' He leaned close and whispered, 'It *is* him though, isn't it?'

'Yes,' said Pippa.

'What about the hidden folk?' asked Taylor.

'They're gone, for now anyway,' she replied. 'Where's Grandpa?'

Taylor and Ollie shared a look of relief then moved aside, letting Pippa and Jed into the living room. Several bookcases and a wooden cabinet had been pushed up against the windows and a dozen candles were flickering in the fireplace, making the room feel cosy despite everything. Grandpa was lying on the sofa with his leg up. He raised his arm and waved when he saw them. 'Pippa! Jed! Thank goodness!' He beckoned Pippa forward and whispered in her ear. 'It *is* him, isn't it?'

'Yes,' said Pippa. She put her arms round his

neck and gave him the biggest hug. 'How's your knee?'

He patted her arm. 'I shan't be running any marathons, but I'll be all right. These two have been taking good care of me.'

Pippa turned to Ollie and Taylor and felt a rush of gratitude. 'Thank you for looking after him,' she said to her friends. She was about to ask them if Jed's changeling was still in the pantry, when they heard vehicles pull on to the driveway.

Jed ran to the front door and drew back the bolts. 'It's Dad!' he shouted.

Their father's coat and trousers were torn and covered in mud. He stepped into the hallway and returned Jed's hug, looking a little taken aback by the sudden show of affection. 'Why's it so dark?' he asked. 'Has there been a power cut?'

'Dad!' cried Pippa.

She limped to him and he pulled her close. 'How are your broken toes? Should you be walking on them?' Before she could explain, he looked her over with concern. 'Why are you both covered in cuts? I thought I saw smoke on our way over here. Is everything all right? Where's Grandpa?'

'He's in the living room. His knee is hurt,' she replied. 'But he's OK.'

'And you're all right?'

'Yes, I'm fine.' Pippa felt her voice tremble. She'd been holding it together for hours and didn't want to break down now.

'Sorry it took me so long to get here,' her father continued. 'The car went into a ditch and a couple stopped and towed me out. They're looking for their son, Ollie, and his cousin. Apparently you play with him sometimes?'

Pippa glanced outside and saw Mr Archer's work van.

'Mum! Dad!' shouted Ollie. He and Taylor squeezed past and ran outside.

Mrs Archer hugged them both. 'Where have you been? We've been worried sick!' She noticed the marks on their hands and faces. 'You're hurt! What happened?'

Ollie's bottom lip trembled. 'We're OK, but I want to go home now.'

Mr Archer patted his son's shoulder. 'We will soon. But first we need to go inside and have a little chat. You and your cousin can tell us how you got those cuts.' He walked up to the children's father and raised his eyebrows. 'That all right with you?'

'Of course,' he replied, frowning at Pippa and Jed as if he'd like an explanation too. 'If you want to go in the kitchen . . .' he said, gesturing for Ollie's parents to go inside. The three grown-ups entered the shadowy room and looked around in stunned silence. 'What on earth happened in here?' asked Dad.

Mr Archer was grim-faced. 'That's what I'd like to know.'

Dad lifted the chairs from the floor and put them straight. He and Mr Archer were about to move the table from in front of the pantry, when Pippa and Taylor shouted at the same time.

'Don't move it!'

'No, don't!'

Dad raised his eyebrows. 'And why's that?'

'We trapped the changeling in there,' explained Ollie.

Mr Archer laughed. 'You trapped *what* in there?'

Ollie's mum gasped and sat down heavily on a chair.

Her husband glanced in her direction then turned his attention back to the pantry.

Pippa wanted to stop him, but at the same time she really wanted to see inside. Jed's changeling hadn't made a sound since they'd returned to the house. Had it fainted, overcome with claustrophobia? Or maybe that's what it *wanted* them to think. 'Be careful,' she warned. 'It looks like Jed, but it's not human. We don't know what it can do.'

'There's one of me?' exclaimed Jed.

Mr Archer laughed again but didn't seem the least amused. He looked irritated and more than a little impatient.

Dad raised his voice. 'Jed, Pippa . . . Can one of you please explain!'

'I'll show you,' said Pippa. 'Help me move the table and stand back.'

The two dads shifted the kitchen table and Pippa removed the chair that was jammed under the door handle. Taking a deep breath, she braced herself and looked inside. But what she saw made no sense.

'Is he there?' called Ollie.

'See for yourself,' said Pippa.

The others rushed forward and peered into the pantry. On the floor was a heap of branches, twigs and moss, along with a few rags. Next to it was a pile of pasta shells.

'I don't understand,' said Taylor.

'He was in there, honest!' protested Ollie.

Pippa shivered. Perhaps her changeling had met the same fate and was now a pile of branches too.

Mr Archer crossed his arms over his chest. 'You kids had better start making sense. I warn you now I'm in no mood for games.'

'You're not going to believe us,' said Pippa.

'And why's that?' he asked.

Ollie put a protective arm around his friend. 'Because it's going to sound crazy and you're going to think we're making it up, but we're not.'

Pippa smiled, grateful for his support. She told them everything: how she'd seen the creature in the glade and how Taylor had helped her with her binoculars. She explained that Jed had been acting strangely and how her real brother had been taken into the stone.

The grown-ups listened wide-eyed as she told them about the hidden folk attacking the house and how she and Jed had set fire to a broom and trapped them underground. She didn't mention the spriggan. She was the only one who'd seen Mamm and their encounter had felt special; it belonged to them alone.

Ollie's mum rubbed her temples and muttered, 'I had a feeling something had disturbed the birds that night, and the way the cats refused to leave the house ... My grandmother told me stories about hidden folk living in these parts. I should have known something wasn't right.'

Mr Archer rolled his eyes then looked back at the children. 'If you think this is funny, I can assure you it's not.'

'Something happened to me too,' Dad said in a quiet voice. 'I saw something run across the road; that's why I went into a ditch.'

Mr Archer frowned. 'You said it was a fox.'

'I said that because I knew how it would sound if I told the truth.'

'And what's that?' asked Mr Archer in a tone that suggested he didn't want to know.

Dad rubbed the back of his neck. 'Trust me, I'm finding this very hard to believe myself.' He took a moment then added, 'I saw a creature like the one Pippa described. And I didn't rip my clothes falling into bushes. Something I couldn't see attacked me.'

Pippa squeezed Dad's hand. It sounded like he'd been having a pretty scary night too.

'Look if you don't believe us, ' said Ollie. He handed the binoculars to Pippa and she rewound the footage and showed it to everyone. She expected the adults to ask lots of questions, but no one said a word.

Eventually Mr Archer broke the silence. 'I don't know how you got this, but things like that can't exist. They just *can't* . . .' He looked at the faces around him then shook his head as if realising it didn't matter whether he believed in such things or not. The evidence was right in front of him.

'I know,' said Ollie. 'But we're telling the truth, Dad. I promise.'

Mr Archer looked unsettled. 'I believe you kids have seen something, but . . .' He peered at the screen. 'Can you go back and zoom in on the stone?'

Pippa did as she was asked.

'The hole doesn't look that big,' he said, rubbing his chin. 'There's some bricks and quick-drying cement in the van. I have a wheelbarrow too. I just need some water.'

'There are some water butts by the shed,' said Pippa.

'And there's another wheelbarrow in the glade,' added Jed.

'Right,' said Mr Archer. 'I don't know what's there, but I say we block up the hole to be on the safe side, unless anyone has any better ideas?'

Pippa looked at her friends, but they shook their heads. Maybe there was a proper way to stop the hidden folk from escaping, some magic or a ritual perhaps, but they'd need to research it. Even if blocking up the hole didn't keep them inside permanently, it seemed worth a shot. 'I think it's a good idea for now,' she said.

Mr Archer nodded and turned to Dad. 'Fancy giving me a hand?'

'Try and stop me,' he replied. 'I just need to check on my dad, and I'll be right with you. Kids, you're to stay indoors. No one is to leave the house while we're gone, OK?'

'I'll make sure they stay inside, don't worry,' said Ollie's mum. She got to her feet, then turned to Pippa and Jed. 'Is there any antiseptic in the house? We need to get your cuts cleaned up, then we can tidy the place and maybe get you something to eat.'

Pippa fetched the first-aid kit from under the sink. It was a relief to have someone take charge and although she wished her mum was there, Mrs Archer was the next best thing.

The following hour passed in a blur of activity. The children lit lots of candles and Ollie's mum saw to their cuts and then swept the floor. It was cold without any glass in the windows, but she got them to fetch some blankets and nailed them up to keep out the draughts.

Once the place looked a little better, they helped Grandpa into the kitchen. He took a seat at the table and seemed in good spirits now the hidden folk were gone. Pippa didn't think she could face eating, but the smell of sausages and buttery mash made her stomach grumble and she realised she was famished.

By the time Dad and Mr Archer returned, dinner was ready to serve. As they ate they talked about everyday things: Taylor's job in the bookshop and the funny customers that came in, Mr Archer getting a contract to work on another new housing estate being built by the forest, Dad's plans for the restaurant. Nobody talked about the hidden folk. It was almost as if they'd made a silent pact.

When it was time for the Archers to leave, Pippa felt sad. She didn't know when they'd get to see Ollie and his cousin again. She didn't even know if Grandpa was going to keep the house. Even if they never came back to this place, she knew Ollie and Taylor would be their friends for life. They'd been through something together they would never forget.

Dad saw their guests to the door and shook Mr Archer's hand. 'Thanks for everything. We must get together again. You're welcome to stay with us in London any time.'

Mr Archer smiled. 'We'd like that. Have a safe journey back.'

Ollie's mum patted Pippa and Jed's father on the arm. 'You've got yourself a good couple of kids there.'

'So have you,' said Dad. He looked over at Pippa and Jed, his face full of pride. 'They've all been incredibly brave. I'm not sure I would have been under the circumstances.'

Jed pulled his shoulders back and stood a little straighter. Pippa smiled. Her brother had helped fight the hidden folk and she was pleased to see him getting the recognition he deserved.

'Ollie's going to give me your phone number,' Taylor said to Pippa as they hugged goodbye. 'Is that OK?'

'Of course!' replied Pippa. 'I'd love to keep in touch. I want to hear how your spooky projects are going.'

Taylor shrugged. 'I've had enough scares; think I'll find a new hobby.'

'Really?' asked Pippa.

'Nah.' Taylor laughed. 'I'm planning to create a website about the supernatural and ask other people to share their experiences. We can't be the only ones.'

'Do you think we should share the video?' asked Pippa.

'It could make us rich and famous,' Taylor said excitedly. 'But if it gets lots of media attention, you can bet someone would open up the stone.'

'You're right,' said Pippa. 'Maybe it's safer to keep it secret for now.'

Ollie barged his cousin aside and hugged Pippa tight, lifting her off the ground. 'Bye, Newt!'

Pippa laughed. 'Bye, Ollie Pops!'

He pulled a face. 'Message me as soon as you get home, yeah?'

'Definitely,' said Pippa. The four of them were going to have a *lot* to talk about.

Ollie and Taylor climbed into the van, and Pippa and Jed waved as it pulled away.

Suddenly it was just them, Dad and Grandpa. Dad closed the front door then put his arms around them. 'It's too late to drive home; I think we should stay here tonight. Grandpa can't walk far, so I'll make him up a bed on the sofa. I'll bring your mattresses down too and we can all sleep together in the living room.'

Pippa didn't like the idea of staying in the house, but the stone was blocked up and she felt safer now that Dad was with them.

'What about Grandpa?' asked Pippa. 'Is he going to come back to London with us?'

'We'll talk about it in the morning,' said Dad.

Their father dragged their mattresses down from their rooms and the children fetched their pillows and duvets. As they made themselves comfy, Pippa found herself thinking about the family camping holiday they'd had last year. They'd had such fun – even Jed had been happy. She reached out and touched his arm.

'Night, Newt,' he whispered.

'Night, Jed.'

As she wriggled under the covers, she wondered if he really was keeping a secret from her. She would speak to him before they left. Things felt better between them and if she waited until they got back home, he might not want to tell her.

She was drifting off to sleep when her thoughts turned to Mamm. If it wasn't for her, they'd still be trapped under the stone. Had she suffered the same fate as her brother, or had she escaped her masters? Mamm said she was going to the place where she'd buried Spring Foot – but where? Pippa decided she would look for her in the morning. Even if it was only to say goodbye, she had to see her again.

29

The next morning Pippa woke early. Light flickered through a gap in the curtains and birdsong filled the room. Rubbing her eyes, she wondered why her mattress was on the floor, then last night's events came back to her and she shuddered.

The door opened and Dad appeared. In his hands was a tray.

'Anyone thirsty?' he asked.

Jed groaned and pulled the covers over his head.

'Sorry,' said Dad. 'I know it goes against the laws of nature to wake a teenager this early, but I want to get going to beat the traffic. I've brought you tea if that helps?' Using his foot, he nudged the sleeping duvet mound that was Jed and was rewarded with a grunt. 'It lives!' laughed Dad.

Grandpa pushed himself up on the sofa. Dipping his head, he grinned at Pippa and mimed tipping a pretend hat. When he noticed her father standing in the room, his smile faltered. 'I would have made tea,' he complained.

'I know, but you need to rest,' said Dad, raising his voice. 'How did you sleep?'

Grandpa rubbed his knee. 'I had a few hours.'

Dad's forehead creased with worry. 'Has the swelling gone down any? If it still hurts I can take you to the doctor's.'

Grandpa waved away his concern. 'That won't be necessary.'

Dad let out a defeated sigh and handed him a tea. 'You know best.'

The day had barely started and Pippa could already sense the tension between them. Dad perched on the arm of the sofa and lowered his head, seemingly deep in thought. 'Dad, I owe you an apology.'

Grandpa almost choked on his tea. 'What did you say? I didn't catch that.'

'I said I owe you an apology! I should have listened when you told me things had been coming into the house. I'm sorry I didn't believe you.'

'Hmm.' Grandpa sniffed. 'Well, perhaps you'll listen to me in future.'

Dad squirmed a little and Pippa had the feeling he was building up to say something else. 'I appreciate you value your independence, but will you think about—'

Grandpa raised his hand, stopping him mid-sentence. 'I know what you're going to say, and I know it makes sense—'

Dad jumped to his feet, his pretence at calm gone. 'Will you let me help you for once? Why is it so hard? I feel bad enough not listening to you and putting the children in danger. Can't you let me do this *one* thing? All I want is to make sure you're OK.'

Grandpa coughed indignantly. 'If you'd let me finish, I was going to say I know it makes sense for me to stay with you for a few days. If you're sure I won't be a burden.'

'Don't start with that *I don't want to be a burden* nonsense . . .'

Pippa glared at her father and he blinked in surprise, realising he hadn't heard properly. 'Oh. So you'll come back with us?'

'Yes,' said Grandpa.

Pippa grinned. She was so relieved and happy she didn't know which of them to hug first. Even Jed surfaced from under the covers and smiled.

'That's sorted then,' said Dad. 'You can stay as long as you want. I'll pack you a bag. Is there anything in particular you want to bring?'

Grandpa pointed to the cabinet, which had been put back in its rightful place. 'There's a couple of photo albums in the bottom drawer I'd like to take. And there's a packet of toffees on my bedside table. Oh, and there's a book I'm reading . . .'

'Should I make a list?' asked Dad.

Grandpa huffed. Pippa pushed off the covers and hugged him. 'I'm so glad you're coming to stay. Tell me what you want and I'll get everything!'

He patted her on the arm. 'You're a good girl.'

Half an hour later everyone was dressed, packed and ready to leave. Grandpa pulled the door closed behind them and Jed helped him walk to the car while Dad put their things in the boot. They didn't talk about what would happen to the house and when he might be back. There would be time enough for making those kinds of decisions once they were all safely in London.

Dad checked his phone, even though he knew there was no reception in the forest.

'As soon as we're back in civilisation, I'll give your mum a call. Hopefully the move went OK. Can you believe we'll be going home to a new house?'

Pippa smiled but then stopped when she saw Jed's face. He looked utterly miserable.

'Can you give us a few minutes?' she asked Dad.

'Sure. Don't take too long though.'

Pippa took Jed's arm and pulled him away.

'What's up?' he asked.

She waited until they'd almost reached the broken oak tree before replying. 'I wanted to talk to you before we got in the car.'

He looked at her doubtfully.

'Please, Jed. I can tell something's wrong. I know you don't want to move house, and I think it has to do with school.'

He looked at his feet.

'I don't like seeing you unhappy. If you tell me, maybe I can help.'

Jed flicked his fringe from his eyes. 'You can't. No one can.'

Pippa nudged him gently. 'Tell me anyway?'

'If you must know, I don't want to move school because I've got friends now.'

Sensing there was more for him to say, she kept quiet.

'The end of last year wasn't good. Some kids were . . .'

'Mean?'

Jed glanced up, his eyes glistening.

'Were they bullying you?' she asked in a quiet voice.

'It's better now. I mean, it still happens, but it's not as bad.'

Pippa tensed her jaw. She wanted to know who had hurt her brother so she could give them a piece of her mind, but now probably wasn't the right time to ask. After a moment, she said, 'Isn't it a good thing, moving schools? You won't have to see any of them again.'

Jed shook his head, his expression a mixture of exasperation and resentment. 'You don't understand because you make friends easily. You don't get anxious and . . .'

'Go on,' said Pippa. 'Tell me.'

'Your face doesn't twitch,' he added glumly.

Pippa touched his arm. She felt terrible for him, but at the same time she was relieved to know what was wrong. It made sense why he blanked her in school. He probably didn't want her to see the other kids giving him a hard time.

'Why didn't you tell Mum and Dad?' she asked.

Jed pulled a face that said, *Do you really have to ask?*

Pippa answered her own question. 'Because Dad would go into school and start yelling.'

'Yup,' said Jed.

Pippa could understand why he'd chosen to do nothing in the hope the bullies left him alone. At the same time, she couldn't help feeling he should speak to their parents. 'I think you should tell Dad,' she said.

'Tell me what?'

The children startled and turned around. Their father was standing right behind them.

When they didn't answer his face crumpled with concern. 'Is it the hidden folk? Have you seen them again? If there's something I should know, please tell me.'

Jed shook his head. 'It's not that.'

Dad looked relieved. 'I thought something terrible had happened from the look on your faces. What is it then?' Neither of them spoke and he glanced from one to the other.

Pippa wanted Dad to know, but it was up to Jed to tell him. Concerned the opportunity might be lost if she didn't say something, she fixed her father with a serious look. 'If Jed tells you, do you promise not to do anything? You just have to listen, OK?'

'I'll do my best.'

Pippa narrowed her eyes at him. She loved her father, but he had a habit of railroading people into doing what he wanted. Like dropping them off with Grandpa when he'd said he didn't want them to stay. Yes, her grandfather could be stubborn and proud, but Dad didn't help matters. 'You can't get angry or tell him what to do,' she continued.

'Yes, Newt,' said Dad. 'I get the message.' He turned

to Jed and softened his voice. 'Whatever it is, I promise not to go off on one.'

Jed looked hesitant and Pippa nodded at him encouragingly.

Keeping his eyes on the ground, Jed told them everything. How a group of kids in his class had been teasing him about his facial tic and taking videos of him and posting them online. How they'd stolen his bag and thrown it over a wall and how they'd taken his clothes when he was getting changed after PE. 'The more they upset me, the worse my twitch became and the more they laughed,' he confided.

Their father listened and didn't say a word, though Pippa could see the hurt on his face and at one point his eyes filled with tears.

'I spent most of my breaks in the library, and that's where I met Jack and Ted. The bullying hasn't stopped entirely, but it's better than it was and now I have mates to stick up for me. I don't want to move schools because what if the kids there laugh at my face? I have friends now, Dad. Proper friends.'

Dad put his hand on Jed's shoulder. 'Thank you for telling me. I knew you were upset about moving, but I had no idea this had been going on. I'm sorry you've been having such a hard time.'

He paused and Pippa watched his face, wondering what he would say next.

'I want you to at least give your new school a try, but if you really don't like it or you have any problems, you can go back to Manning Park.'

Jed's face brightened. 'Really?'

Dad raised his hands. 'It's a long commute, but if you're happy to sit on the train for an hour . . .'

Jed hugged Dad.

'If anything happens – at *either* school – I want you to tell me or your mum. I promise we won't do anything without checking with you first. But I can't let you be bullied.'

Jed nodded. 'OK.'

'Right,' said Dad. 'Now that's sorted, shall we go home?'

Pippa glanced at the broken oak tree. There was one more thing she needed to do. 'Can I have a few more minutes?'

Dad rolled his eyes and smiled. 'Go on then. But be quick.'

As they walked back to the car, Dad put his arm around Jed and she noticed her brother lean into him. Watching them gave her a warm glow inside.

Turning to the tree, Pippa searched the long grass. She was certain she'd seen Mamm here, watching them on their way back to the house yesterday. She was about to give up and return to the car when she spotted something. A hessian sack lay next to a pile of branches, moss and rotting fruit. To anyone else it would seem like nothing, yet Pippa immediately dropped to her knees. She gently nudged the hessian sack and two little acorns rolled out.

'I'm sorry,' she whispered to the ground. 'I was hoping you might have got away, or maybe . . .' Pippa didn't know what she hoped would happen, only that Mamm would survive somehow. She'd said it would not end well for her. She'd known the consequences, yet she'd still helped them. She'd given her life so that she and Jed would be safe.

Pippa picked up a couple of branches and wondered whether she should bury them. There was so much about Mamm and her life that she didn't know and would never understand. Hoping she was doing the right thing, she used her hands to scrabble a hole in the earth. Then she placed the cloth and other remains inside and covered them with dirt.

Wiping her eyes, she whispered a few heartfelt words. Then she hurried back to the car and got inside. Dad started the engine and Pippa turned and looked out of the rear window. Her chest ached. She felt so many things – relieved to be leaving, yet sad and thankful to Mamm at the same time.

Grandpa was in the front seat, and Jed was in the back holding his Switch and wearing his earbuds.

'What are you playing?' she asked.

He pulled out one of his earbuds and raised his eyebrows.

'Your game . . . what are you playing?' she repeated.

'Sonic. Want to try?' Jed handed the earbud to her and she placed it in her ear. 'Push this control, here, and Sonic will go faster. Push this and he'll jump.'

Pippa took the console from him. 'OK, but don't expect me to be any good!' She moved the controls and a twinkly noise sounded in her ear as Sonic collected a golden ring.

'See, you're a natural,' said Jed.

He tried to take his Switch back, but she held on to it.

Nudging her leg, he playfully thumped her on the arm. 'Dad, will you tell Newt to give my game back!'

Dad shook his head and laughed. 'You two don't change!'

Pippa handed the console over and watched as Jed expertly whizzed through the screens. She waited until he was about to win then jabbed him in the ribs, putting him off. When it was her turn to play, he pulled funny faces and made her giggle so much that she couldn't concentrate. It was going to be a long journey home, but she was glad she had her brother to laugh with and annoy. Just like always.

30

Mamm Spriggan resides in the earth, but she does not sleep and she does not dream. Her essence is elsewhere: a whisper carried on the wind, a fading echo of a half-forgotten memory. She is a shadow of awareness drifting silently on the air.

A familiar voice speaks and like a kite snagged on a tree she is caught fast, her interest tethered to a single place and time.

'I don't know if you're there, or if you can hear me,' says the girl. 'But I want to say thank you. My name is Pippa Newton. I'm hoping we can be friends.'

A single salty tear falls to the ground and a flicker of energy sparks through the soil as the quickening takes hold. A branch shifts in the earth, connecting with another, and then a pine cone turns slightly and two acorns roll towards one another. Like a seed reaching for the sun, Mamm feels the urge to remake herself. This time, the kernel at the core of her being doesn't throb with hate. It is the bond forged between human and spriggan that summons her into being – the gentle calling of a kindred spirit, a friend.

Acknowledgements

Thanks to my ever-supportive agent Amber Caravéo, and my fantastic editors: Felicity Alexander, Matt Ralphs and Georgina Mitchell.

Thanks also to the kind beta readers who gave me early feedback on the story, including my mum. Love you.

Rachel Burge works as a freelance feature
writer and has written for a variety
of websites, including BBC Worldwide,
Cosmo, and MTV. She lives in East Sussex
with her partner and son.

WHISPERING HOLLOW

RACHEL BURGE

WHISPERING HOLLOW

WELBECK
CHILDREN'S BOOKS

WELBECK CHILDREN'S BOOKS

First published in Great Britain in 2024 by Welbeck Children's Books,
an imprint of Hachette Children's Group

1 3 5 7 9 10 8 6 4 2

A CIP catalogue record for this book
is available from the British Library.

ISBN 978 1 804 53617 9

Typeset in Migration Sans ITC Std by Jouve (UK), Milton Keynes
Printed and bound in Great Britain by Clays Ltd, Elcograf S.p.A.

The paper and board used in this book
are made from wood from responsible sources.

Welbeck Children's Books
An imprint of
Hachette Children's Group
Part of Hodder & Stoughton Limited
Carmelite House
50 Victoria Embankment
London EC4Y 0DZ

An Hachette UK Company
www.hachette.co.uk

www.hachettechildrens.co.uk